"This is a serious book, no question, about matters of faith and love and mortality, yet it is also playful, sardonic, silly, chatty, and sometimes curt. And while this work is clearly reminiscent of the best of its kind, in a strange and intoxicating universe that includes writers from Vonnegut to Barry Yourgrau, Egerton's take is all his own." —*Rain Taxi*

"Rarely do stories complement each other so well as in this bizarre collection, which is at once darkly tragic, hoarsely satirical, exuberantly hilarious, and deeply moving. Egerton's art is driven by a playfulness which rings throughout all these gems, but it far from undercuts the serious. The variety of genres in this volume, from traditional short stories to blistering flash fiction, fairy tales to self-referential annotations, are all peppered with an abundance of moods and attitudes. The stories strike you with horror, form lumps in your throat, and make you smirk." —*Curled Up with a Good Book*

PRAISE FOR
Everyone Says That at the End of the World

"A brainy, often riotous, ultimately moving *Cat's Cradle* for our time peopled with reluctant seekers of spiritual nourishment who might have stepped from the pages of Flannery O'Connor." —*Kirkus*

"People at the coffee shop were actually staring at me—I don't think they fully believed that a book could make a person laugh that hard. Egerton has written a expansive novel that is generous enough to cover the end of the world, and the beginning, and a good number of the key points in between, and filled it with warmth, intelligence, wisdom, and humor—a personal and universal cosmology that made me laugh and think and feel and laugh some more. I think this is a future classic, and people will be reading this book decades from now. I know I will." —Charles Yu, author of *How to Live Safely in a Science Fictional Universe*

"In this expansive, funny, touching epic—part travelogue, part quest narrative— Egerton offers up a Texan love letter generous enough to include even the nutria." —Amelia Gray, author of *Threats*

PRAISE FOR *The Book of Harold*

"A lively and beautifully crafted novel about the anguish of belief."—*Kirkus*

"I love every word that Owen Egerton writes or utters and *The Book of Harold* bumps my admiration up to a new level. It takes a brave author to attempt satire these days. But it takes Owen Egerton to make it the wise, hilarious, finely-observed, and, ultimately, compassionate ring-tailed delight that *The Book of Harold* is."
—Sarah Bird, author of *The Gap Year*

"Only Owen Egerton can create a new religion around a former computer salesman and make you want to up and take a pilgrimage to Austin with the rest of the Haroldians. Egerton has the gift of walking that fine line between hilarity and heart with grace. Follow."
—Elizabeth Crane, author of *All This Heavenly Glory*

"An engaging exploration of everything ridiculous, horrible, and beautiful that humanity has ever been given or invented about religion."
—*The Hipster Book Club*

HOW

BEST TO

AVOID

DYING

HOW BEST TO AVOID DYING

{ STORIES }

OWEN EGERTON

SOFT SKULL PRESS
AN IMPRINT OF COUNTERPOINT
BERKELEY

Library of Congress Cataloging-in-Publication Data
Egerton, Owen.
[Short stories. Selections]
How to best avoid dying : stories / Owen Egerton.
pages cm
ISBN 978-1-59376-522-4
I. Title.
PS3605.G47A6 2014
813'6—dc23
2013026635

Cover design by Matt Dorfman
Interior design by Tabitha Lahr

SOFT SKULL PRESS
An imprint of COUNTERPOINT
1919 Fifth Street
Berkeley, CA 94710
www.softskull.com

Printed in the United States of America
Distributed by Publishers Group West

10 9 8 7 6 5 4 3 2 1

For
Nathan Altman
a friend and a writer who died young

"God's not ready for you," the walls say.

"Fine," I reply, "because I'm not ready for him either."

"But keep working on your death song," warn the walls.

"Oh, I will. I work on it every day."

—Albert Huffstickler
Working on my Death Chant

CONTENTS

HOW

BEST TO

AVOID

DYING

SPELLING

"Your word is *ambrosial.*"

"*Ambrosial?*"

"*Ambrosial.*"

"Can you use it in sentence?"

"The talented chef prepared an *ambrosial* dessert for the party."

"A-M-B-R...O-S...I-A...L"

"That is correct."

"Yippie!"

The crowd cheers. Sally always says "Yippie." She says it's her "calling card." Pretty crappy calling card, if you ask me. She's also big into building the drama. Pausing, sweating a little. Like *ambrosial.* Easy word. She knew it straightaway, but she has to add some tension, as if the Pit weren't enough. She's only eight, a year younger than me, and already a showman. You grow up fast in the Bee.

Only five of us left. Sally, Peter, Wilma, Shaka and me. Always more girls than boys near the end. We're just better.

No one has missed in a while, which means the words will get harder. They like to have a miss every five people or so, so even if this is only round four, they'll add some round five words to spice things up.

Peter stands up, walks to the Spot. He's got nice dark hair and green eyes. He can be really funny too. He peers out into the darkness, knowing there are thousands watching in the arena, more on television. He swallows. And from the darkness comes the voice.

"Your word is *pulchritudinous.*"

"*Pulchritudinous?*"

"*Pulchritudinous.*"

Peter coughs.

"P-U-L…C-H…R." He pauses. This isn't for show. That's not Peter's style. He's in trouble, so he's taking his time. Once you say a wrong letter, you can't go back "I-T…U-D…" Oh, man. He's sweating up a storm. Oh, man, oh man. "I-N-O-S."

"Bing!" The wrong bell.

"No. P-U-L-C-H-R-I-T-U-D-I-N-O-U-S."

The audience gasps. Peter looks sad for just a moment, then smiles at the hidden crowd, does a cute little shrug and an exaggerated bow. He told me he'd do this when he goes out. Wants to be remembered. The crowd laughs at his spunk and gives him a round of applause. Then the Pit opens beneath him and he falls.

God, the smell is awful. Like rot and poop. We spellers can't see inside the Pit, but we can hear him land with a kind of splat and then the crunching starts. Slow. The audience can see. There's a wide window below the stage with a perfect view into the Pit. They always gasp and ooo and ahh. Surprised each time. Peter screams for a little longer than most. Then the Pit closes and they call for the next speller.

I'll miss Peter. I liked him. Not in a boyfriend kind of way. Just a friend. No time for boyfriends. Too much studying. I want to be the world's best speller. America needs me. Ever since we lost Hawaii to Korea in the Spelling Bee of the Pacific, we've been the laughingstock of the world.

Wilma is wearing a pink flowery dress. She's the prettiest girl in the Bee, especially since Sue went out in round two. But, like Coach says, "Looks don't spell."

"Your word is *Polywomack*."

"*Polywomack*?"

"*Polywomack*."

"Can you use it in a sentence?"

"No."

"Origin, please?"

"American Council of Nu-Words."

They usually don't bring in Nu-Words until round six. Poor Wilma. I hate Nu-Words.

"Could you repeat the word?"

"*Polywomack*."

She's buying time. She's trying to decide if the Nu-Word is spelled like it sounds or if it has some silent letter or trick or something.

"P-O-L-Y-W-O-M-A-C-K. Polywomack."

"That is correct."

The crowd gives a hoot. Wilma is a crowd favorite. She dresses right, smiles right, spells right. Cute and competent.

I hate her. Me, I'm all spell. I get up, I spell. End of story. No show, no pretty dress, no little waves. Just give me the word and get out of my way. Coach says I could learn from Wilma, learn to use the positive vibes of the crowd to feed my head. But I don't need them. I'm a badass speller. B-A-D-A-S-S.

Shaka stands and shuffles to the microphone looking like she might shatter into a hundred pieces. She is shy as hell. Afraid of all those eyes she can't see. She'd probably be the champ if she weren't so afraid all the time. She rocks the in-class scrimmages, but the pressure of the real thing, the crowd, the Pit, all get to her.

"Your word is *clematises.*"

"*Clematises?*" Her voice breaks a little. She's going to choke. Better here than in the Bee for Oil Reserves of Canada.

"C…" she takes a long pause, likes she's frozen. "L?" Oh, this bad. The Pit opens just a crack below her feet. She's trembling something awful. "E…" she squeaks it out. The Pit crack opens a little more. We can smell it, see the heat is rising out of it. The crowd must be on the edge of their seats. "M-A-T…" The crack beneath her spreads, she's got a foot on either side, her legs making a giant upside down V. There's a trickle of pee running down her leg. That's awful. Just awful. "I-S-E…" Come on, Shaka. Finish it up. "S. Clematises."

"That is correct." The crowd cheers. The Pit closes. Shaka bites her lips and starts to cry a little. Jesus, she looks bad. So she has another week, but after pissing myself in front of a billion people I think I'd rather the Pit.

Then it's me. I walk to the Spot. I don't think about the Pit, or Peter, or Wilma's dress, or Shaka's pee, or anything. I just wait for the word.

"Your word is *ebullient*."

Easy peasy. I guess they like me. "A…"

Oh, God. It's not A. It's E.

Oh, God. I can't go back. "B…" What do I do? Once I'm done spelling the Pit opens. Do I spell the rest of *ebullient* or do I spell some other word? Do I spell the right word wrong or the wrong word right? Oh, man. "A-L…" I glance behind me. All the spellers know. No one is smiling, not even Wilma. "I-E-N…" You know who doesn't know? The crowd. They have to wait on some wrong bell to tell them how to spell. Man. The letters are getting furry. "A-T-E."

"Bing!"

The Pit opens under me and I fall, but my pants snag on a corner, and I'm hanging head down. I see the crowd through the window. All staring at me with egg eyes. Their faces are paste. My pants start to tear, I drop down a few inches. From above I hear Shaka wailing. Below me in dark I can see the wet eyes of a hundred pigs. I can hear them crawling on each other. I'll be falling soon. My pants rip a little more. I wish this moment would last forever.

Habits die hard. For thirty-four years I was a Waffle House secret inspector. In fact, I was the top secret inspector. I traveled to every Waffle House in the nation and trained hundreds of others. My unofficial title was Über-Inspector. But then my wife died and I suddenly grew old and they asked me to retire. That was six months ago, but my eyes still catch it all. The batter crust on the menu, the cracked tile three from the register, the radio playing instead of the jukebox. Minor infractions. Nothing I'd report to the main office. Just notes for the manger in my report. I would never meet him. He can never know my face. Secrecy is key. I used to take notes with a pen the size of a toothpick on a notepad the size of a credit card. But I've turned in my tiny pen and pad. Still, I can't help but think what I *would* have written.

NOTE: WAITRESS "HILLARY." SHIRT STAINED AND UNTUCKED. PANTS RUMPLED.

Hillary is obese. Very obese. The front roll of her belly rests on my table. Her hair is an unnatural red, heated coil red. It sticks out from her scalp like wires. She is wearing makeup, but she is not wearing it well. It looks as if it has been applied in the dark by a drunk child.

I don't judge people based on physical beauty. But Hillary is unclean and that's a bad trait for a food server. She also has a problem with mucus. She places a glass of water down and drags her flabby, wet nostrils along her uniform's sleeve. I'm disgusted, but my face reveals nothing. I am a spy.

"Anything to drink?" she asks. Her voice is pleasant enough. Softer than I'd expected.

"I'll have a decaf coffee, please." Under the table I press start on my stopwatch. The beverage should reach the custom-

WAFFLE

No matter the city, no matter the state, the smell is there to greet me. The thick scent of bacon and coffee and batter. No matter where I am, Waffle House smells like home.

I arrive at 3:23 AM.

"Good morning," the waitresses and cook say.

NOTE: GREETING COULD USE MORE VERVE. FLOOR AT ENTRANCE STICKY.

Store #AZ254 sits just off of Interstate 10 on the outskirts of Phoenix. It's the last one I'll see this far west. I'm driving to my daughter's house in San Diego. No Waffle Houses there. Only sugar-soaked IHOPs and God-forsaken Denny's.

I sit down at the second to last booth in the non-smoking section.

NOTE: BLINDS NEED DUSTING. CASA DE WAFFLE HOT SAUCE ECLIPSED BY A.1. SAUCE. SYRUP CONTAINER NEEDS TOPPING UP.

er within a minute and a half. Add an extra fifteen seconds if the order is hot cocoa.

I watch Hillary clop back behind the counter. And stop. Not stop to help a customer or wipe the counter or reshuffle the sweeteners. No, Hillary just stops and leans against the counter, nearly snapping a menu holder. She gazes up at the ceiling and sways slightly to the radio. A minute passes. No decaf. A minute and a half. She's still swaying. Three minutes. I tap the table. At five minutes I stop my watch. Sometime later Hillary blinks, brushes some of her head wires, and returns to my table.

"You know what you want to eat?"

"I haven't received my coffee yet."

"You want coffee?"

"Decaf."

She swivels around and heads back. She looks tempted to stop again, but doesn't.

As in every Waffle House, there are two distinct coffee pots. Black handle for regular. Orange handle for decaffeinated. Hillary grabs the black handle, pours a cup and returns to my table.

"Is that decaf?" I ask.

She nods.

"Because I'm allergic to caffeine and if it's not decaf my heart will explode and I will die."

"I'm allergic to walnuts."

My hands twitch.

"Any thing to eat?" she asks. I order the All-Star Special.

"Stumpy," she yells. "We need an ASS."

Stumpy, a short black cook hovering over the grill, raises his hand, which isn't there. In place of the hand is a spatula duct-taped to the stump. I watch him. He's fast. He's good. I relax and sip my coffee. I'm not really allergic to caffeine. Just that the doctor recommends I give it up. My heart is not what it was. Had an incident a month back. Couldn't move my arms for two days. So good to taste real coffee again. Oh lord, I used to drink coffee. Black, full-fledged coffee. On the road for weeks at a time, sitting in Waffle Houses like this one, downing coffee and thinking out comments like proverbs.

A W.H. IS ONLY AS STRONG AS ITS 4:30 AM HASHBROWNS.

IF A WAITRON DOESN'T CARE ABOUT THE WAFFLE, HOW CAN THEY EXPECT A CUSTOMER TO CARE ABOUT THE WAFFLE?

ENCOURAGE SMILES. THEY'RE MORE POWERFUL THAN SALT.

Waffle Houses are magic. Eclectic gatherings. It's a quarter till four and look at these wanderers who have found each other. The drunk stewing at the counter, the Hispanic couple cooing in booth three, the teenagers daring each other to French kiss spoonfuls of ketchup. This is life. This is America. And I'm leaving it all behind.

My daughter has a room waiting for me in San Diego.

"Come on Dad, we want to have you."

"I'm fine on my own."

"Dad, Mom's not there to take care of you and you're not a healthy man."

"I'm fine."

Wendy should have had kids. Instead she and her Hamilton jet-setted around the globe until her womb dried up. Her mother told her, "If you don't start soon, you'll be too old to enjoy them." But for Wendy it was always, "We're enjoying each other right now. Give us some time." No one could have guessed her womb had the shelf life of a peach. She cried on the phone when the doctor told her. Called up, asked to speak to her mother, and wept for forty-five minutes. And now she wants me to play baby.

The All-Star Special includes two eggs, one waffle, four strips of bacon, grits, and toast. It should arrive at the table in six to nine minutes. Stumpy prepares a plate in seven minutes and thirty-four seconds. Well done, Stumpy. Hillary brings it to the table—not careless, but clumsy. As she walks the eggs slide into the grits, but she's trying and she's smiling. I'll give her that, she smiles.

Runny eggs, soft waffle, shiny bacon. I'm happy. I like Waffle Houses to work. I like to write STELLAR at the top of my report. I like the basics to be covered so a store can go deeper. Moving beyond "Was the water glass refilled?" to "What was the true motivation of the waiter pouring the water?"

I enjoy every bite, saving the waffle for last. I'm ready to add the perfect amount of Whipped Spread and syrup and gobble it up while it's still hot, but when I open up my tub of Whipped Spread I find an unpleasant surprise.

NOTE: MELTED SPREAD.

It's a tub of yellow liquid, little white globs floating like scum in an over-used hotel hot tub. I motion for Hillary, who is staring at the air. She sees me and waddles over.

"More coffee?" she asks.

"Can I have another tub of butter? This one is melted." Notice I call it butter. All part of the disguise. Anyone who knows Waffle House knows the Whipped Spread is about as close to butter as Alabama is to Asia. Personally, I prefer the spread. Perfect for waffles.

Hillary is on her way back to my table with a fresh tub when the phone rings. She squeals and hops to the phone. It's the fastest I've seen her move since I arrived.

"Hello, Waffle House," she says. She nods, then covers the mouthpiece. "Stumpy, it's the radio people again."

"Oh, my," says Stumpy, turning from his half-grilled hash browns. The drunk at the counter gives a loud whoop.

"They want to know the phrase that pays."

My waffle is cooling.

"I don't know any phrases," Stumpy shrugs.

"We don't know any phrases," Hillary says into the phone. I touch my waffle. Definitely cooling. Hillary nods some more, uttering "a-huh" with each drop of her chin. My last waffle before San Diego is getting cold. I am about to stand and retrieve my own spread when she hangs up and skips over to my table. She hands me my tub and gives the sweetest little curtsy. My anger vanishes and I smile.

"Radio people?" I ask.

"They've been calling us for the past hour. It's their morning show."

"It's four AM."

"They start real early."

"Is it the station we're listening to?"

"Yep, yep, yep."

"Why didn't we hear you?"

She looks at me with what I can only presume is some kind of pity. "They pre-record it," she says.

I nod and return to my waffle. I open my new spread and find it too is liquid.

"Excuse me," I grab Hillary by the sleeve. "This is also melted."

"Yeah," she frowns. "We keep them by the grill." She walks away.

Funny. When Hillary frowned she had the slightest resemblance to my wife. Very slight. My wife wasn't as big, my wife had nearly perfect teeth, my wife was always carefully groomed, but she was a redhead. Hair like a sunset. Rich red when we met, mellowing as the years passed, yellows sneaking in and finally a light shade of blue over orange. I was out of town when she died. The cable man found her in the garden. I miss her.

Hillary comes by and takes my half-eaten waffle. I don't stop her.

How did my skin get so spotted? So loose? It's dying on my bones.

"Anything else?"

I look up. Hillary is waiting, doodling on her pad. I take a deep breath. "Yes, please," I say. My last meal at a Waffle House. It needs the perfect ending. "A hot slice of apple pie and a cold scoop of vanilla ice cream."

"No apple pie," she says without looking from her doodles. "I think we're out."

"Can you check?"

"I did a minute ago," she says. "We're out."

"Then why did you say you think?"

She looks up from her pad. "It's a figure of speech. Like a metaphor."

"Like a metaphor?"

"Would you like pecan?"

"I want apple."

"No apple. Just pecan."

I order pecan. She brings it, smiling again, but I no longer find it pleasant. The pecan pie tastes like sticky chalk. Hard to swallow. I chew slowly. I try to calm myself. My doctor says no losing my temper. I'm too old to afford anger.

"More coffee?" she asks. I could kill her. "Or another slice of pie?" I could pour syrup down her throat until she drowns.

The phone rings and Hillary squeals, drops my check and scampers off.

I try another bite. Paper and sugar.

"They say I should stand on a table," Hillary says to Stumpy, the phone again pressed to her ear. "They say they're watching somewhere outside. They want me to lift my shirt, Stumpy."

"You can't see titties on the radio."

"Stumpy, it's five thousand dollars."

"I don't know. You could lose—"

But it's too late. Hillary climbs up on the table of the booth next to mine, unbuttons her shirt and out flop her breasts. Dear God. Pink, strained flesh popping from the sides of a tan mesh bra. It's as if two shaved possums are hammocked and hibernating on her chest. The teenagers gasp, the drunk claps, Stumpy hides his eyes with his one good hand.

Hillary giggles, rebuttons her shirt, and bounces back to the phone.

"What are they saying?" Stumpy asks.

"I don't know. They're laughing," Hillary says. "They hung up. I don't understand." She puts down the phone. "I think they said something mean." Her face is a flustered red. "I wonder how I get my money?"

My anger is gone. It's just too sad. I abandon my pecan pie, walk up to the register, and hand Hillary a twenty dollar bill and my check. I avoid looking at her. I avoid thinking about her. I just want to be outside, driving away.

"Here's your change," she says, no embarrassment, no shame in her tone. It makes everything worse. I'm looking up to tell her to keep the change when I notice that, right next to the register, on a plate, under a glass lid sits an untouched, genuine, Waffle House apple pie. And there's Hillary's chubby fist handing me crumpled bills.

"I take it back," I say. "I do not like the Waffle House." My voice is loud. The couple looks up. "I do not enjoy your smells, your grimy menus. I despise your unclean lavatories, your tumorous steaks, your powdered hot cocoa." The drunk is leaning away. Stumpy is forgetting to flip an egg. "And you," I yell, pointing a shaking finger at Hillary. "You are not going to win any money, you stupid thing. Thing! So mop the entrance floor, turn down the music, and keep the goddamned spread in the fridge."

The door dings open.

"Good morning," Stumpy says weakly, keeping his eyes on me. I turn to the door. Two men walk in carrying a life sized pink cow with the words KLOL CASH COW painted on the side.

"We're here to give away some mooooney!" shouts one of the men into a wireless microphone.

"Oh my God! Oh my God! Oh my God!" Hillary leaps up and down, her body jiggling in copious waves. The other man runs through the store high-fiving the customers and staff, stopping just short of Stumpy. It takes both men to hoist Hillary up on the back of the Cash Cow. They hand her a wad of cash and snap some photos.

"Mooooney," says the Cash Cow.

Stumpy turns up the radio and pumps his arms in the air.

"The Waffle House is a rockin'," yells one DJ into his microphone. "What's the station that pays, Hillary?"

"I don't even know!" she yelps.

Hillary is happy. A goofy, doughy ball of joy. Why can't I feel happy for her? Why do I find myself wishing the plastic cow would collapse under her weight or that the DJs would snap the money back and laugh at her naïveté?

Stumpy is weeping behind the counter. People are cheering and laughing and toasting Hillary with coffee cups and juice glasses. Hillary is chanting, "Thank you, radio people! Thank you, radio people!"

I squeeze past the Cash Cow and leave.

It is still more night than morning. But the sky is growing paler. I notice the Waffle House sign is glowing above me.

NOTE: A AND SECOND F NEED NEW BULBS.

I climb into my car and start the engine. Glancing in my rearview mirror, I can't see the Cash Cow, it's below the window, but I see Hillary. She's galloping. Waving an arm above her head like a rodeo star.

As I pull out of the parking lot and head west, I imagine Hillary chasing after me, galloping her Cash Cow out of the Waffle House, through the parking lot and into the traffic of Interstate 10, pursuing me all the way to California, hollering like a Valkyrie, with a pot of coffee in one hand and a slice of apple pie in the other, daring me every moment of every mile not to feel ecstatic about being alive in this world.

COLD

NIGHT

ALLIGATOR

You want me to turn the electric fence off? Really? You want in? You redneck fucktards. There're alligators in here, royally pissed, cold alligators, you know that? They'd eat your dogs easy.

You cut off our heat, our water. You pump spotlights and techno music at us so no one sleeps for three weeks and the alligators go weird and bite the mud. Your dogs barking blood. Of course we turned on the fence.

And why? Because we're some crazy cult? You want crazy people? You made crazy people. You made Eve 9 crazy and she was as sane as it gets. You put something in her eyes I've never seen.

And we loved you. We prayed for your turd-dimple town, prayed for your lame lives. But you hated us the moment we arrived, right when we drove down Main. You stared at our bus, pinching your noses at the smell of veggie oil. We waved and you didn't. We smiled and you didn't. I told Troy right then, "They hate us."

"All the more reason to love them," Troy said.

What an asshole.

I know in here they think he's a god and out there you think he's a demon. But he's my brother, I know him. He's just an asshole. You freaks called in the Feds for some harmless asshole with good people skills and a soft heart and some weird ideas about reptiles. He used to say he loved the world and everyone in it. I said look at history, Socrates to MLK, love the world and it comes to kill you. Thanks a hell of a lot for proving me right, you maggot dicks.

You know what our philosophy is? Do you know the ideology you're trying wipe out? *Answer suffering with love. Open your self to beauty.* That's it. That's what we say together at the end of each day, what we say to each other each morning. That's what we believe, love and beauty. And fucking. We fuck a lot. We do. That's why I joined. That's why most of us joined. At least the guys. You think that's shallow? Do you? Fuck you.

My brother started a cult in our shitty Jacksonville apartment. You think I stuck around because I thought he was prophet? He was chemistry grad student, for chrissakes. I was playing Wii on the couch and he said it for the first time, said our creed: *Answering suffering with love. Open your self to beauty.*

"Hmm," I said and went back to Wii.

Troy made his Facebook status *Answer suffering with love. Open your self to beauty.* Some people *liked* the shit out of it. Not many, but some. He invited folks over for spaghetti and talk. I listened, mocked my brother when he needed reality, reminded him that most people would crap on his love.

"Because they're suffering. So love them!"

More and more came every week. Pasta, teachings, and, after a while, sex. Not crazy orgies, just one-on-one, old fashioned fucking, okay. When we make love we believe we're literally *making* love. And the world needs love. So were fucking for a better world. Are you fucking for a better world? No? So shut the fuck up.

Hell, I bet Eve 9 and I alone have made enough love to save the world three times over. Fay, that was her name before. Fay Blakes. She walked into Troy's apartment with some ass-faced boyfriend during one of the early dinners. She had this pageboy haircut and tiny, happy breasts like those oversized Hersheys Kisses they sell around Valentines, only not as pointy. The boyfriend left. She stayed.

She has this floating way about her. She wears the collar of her gray jumpsuit just a little bent. So fucking cute. And when the Family stands facing east, waking the dawn with our collective sigh, I sneak near her just to smell her morning breath.

Troy saw the alligator farm for sale online. Cheap, run down, sick gators, in shit-shape like everything else in this town. "The northernmost alligator farm in America!"? Who the fuck thought that up? Missouri is like the arctic to alligators. Without care, they'll die.

We thought we could make it paradise. I remember that first day here, Troy standing on the porch of the big house where we built all the bunks, gazing at us, beaming.

"Answer suffering with love."

"Yes!" we cheered.

"Open yourself to beauty."

"Yes!"

"Eat an alligator egg every day."

"Yee…sure!"

Okay, Troy feels alligator eggs have special spiritual prop-
erties. Like Omega 3 for the soul. Ah, shut up. Half of you eat
the flesh of Jesus once a week. So if you think the gator stuff is
weird, fuck you.

We abandoned the old world, the old names. I became
Adam 2. Troy named himself Proto-Adam the Holy.

Holy my ass. Little secret. As a kid he used to almost constantly spray the toilet seat with piss. It got so bad mom made
a rule that he had to sit down every time he went. It stuck. He'd
never admit it, but to this day Proto-Adam the Holy pees sitting down.

We spent our days caring for the alligators and showing
tourists around. In the evenings we talked about love, suffering, beauty. Dinner was pasta and alligator eggs and when the
sun went down we fucked until our calves hurt. Best years of
my life. Maybe anyone's life.

We had babies. Jesus, I must have fathered half a dozen.
Eve 9 had the first, the first baby born to the Family. Fay yelling,
the women gathering near, the pain, the growls, then a child.
Troy said this is our creed, suffering and beauty together. Little
Eve 43. I like to think she's mine. There's no way to know. That's
the point. You know, one belongs to all and all belong to one.

Tiny baby. The love we had been making was crying
on Eve 9's chest. And Eve 9, Fay, exhausted and so happy, hot
sweat beading on her forehead.

Take my word, the worst thing you could do in a sex cult
is fall in love with one person. The aim is to share each other,
give yourself to all, belong to no one individual. But I wanted
to belong to her. And her to me. We have a rule that you can't

sleep with the same person more than twice in a row. I'd spend two nights with Eve 9, hurry off and get handjob from Eve 12 or something, and scurry back to Eve 9. And in the sack, which is anywhere but the sack since we all sleep in a bunkroom, so in the shed, or laundry room or hatchery, when Eve 9 gets really excited she makes this high pitched squeal like an injured rabbit. I love that.

You know where Eve 9 is now? She's curled up in a corner shaking in the cold, half starved. I told you, just him, take him and leave the Family alone. You sped up with sirens on a dozen cop cars, waving a warrant like a battle flag. Of course we closed the gates, of course we electrified the fences. How do you expect people to react when you come to take their babies away?

We never should have sent our kids to your schools. Never. Troy said to love a society, you have to be present in that society. So we sent them. You hated our children as much as you hated us. It wasn't just that they were all Adams and Eves, not just the smaller gray jumpsuits, it was that they didn't know *Iron Man*, didn't recognize Sponge Bob on the lunch boxes. It irked you. You hated them so much you called it concern. Prayed they could be delivered and transformed into less freaky, less hateable creatures. But you could do nothing, and you cursed your own laws that allowed for freedom of wrong religions.

Troy taught our children that the smirks, the bullies, the unspoken disgust had no power over them.

"Those who hate are suffering. Answer suffering with love. How can someone you love ever really hurt you?" he said. "Now have another egg."

I could have told him he was wrong. I was his grounded counselor. I saw you for the puss sacks you are. But I was too busy sticking with Eve 9. I lied to her about other women. I swore I was fucking everyone. But it was just her.

Troy knew. He came to me. I was feeding antibiotics to a sedated alligator.

"Brother," he said, which didn't mean much. He calls everyone brother or sister. "Let's talk about Eve 9."

I smirked and asked him if he'd squat a piss recently.

"I'm taking her tonight. I'm doing this for you."

I stared.

"Open yourself to beauty, brother. In time you can be with her again," he said.

"Troy," I said. "Please don't do this."

"That's not my name," he said. The gator started to wake.

He was good to his word, he always is. That night he took her into his room, the only private room on the Farm. I lay in my bed, eyes on the bunk above me, twenty feet from his door. Everything in me bubbled. Every alligator egg I'd ever swallowed trying to squeeze back up my throat. I closed my eyes and counted breaths. Then I heard the cries of a dying rabbit. I walked away. I walked off the farm.

That's why I hate him. Even more than you shit worms. If you had taken him it would have been fine. But you made it hell in here. No food, no water. Bull horning through the fence that if we loved our children we'd send them out, get them to safety, said they'd be with their brothers and sisters, the ones who left for school and never came back. You made our world so unsafe and so hellish that we listened. We lined up the little Eves and Adams and sent them walking out to you, knowing you'd keep them, knowing you'd stuff them with Lucky Charms and church hymns and wash all their life away. We kissed them. We touched their matted hair. Told them we'd see them soon, knowing we wouldn't. They promised us with hot tears that they would walk in love, saying how can someone they love ever really hurt them? Troy ripped hair from his face.

Then one of you shot an alligator. What the fuck was that? What, it got a little too close to the fence? They're endangered, for God's sake. It wasn't even a clean shot. It took hours to die.

You know what we did? We had a funeral for it. Do you get that? We love the alligators. Troy ceremonially skinned it. He's wearing it. He's creeping around the swamps calling himself the Resurrected Gator Lord, whispering mad plans. And I don't blame him. *You're* the ones who brought the crazy.

The night Troy took Eve 9 I walked an hour toward town. I found a roadside bar and sat on an open stool. I didn't have any money. None of us have money.

I wanted to be drunk, to root for the Cowboys on TV, to go to sleep in a big bed alone with Eve 9 and have babies and name them Rachael and Amber. Then one of you came up to me. An old man with a splotchy face. I expected him to insult me or push me. I wanted him to. Instead he bought me a beer. My first in twelve years. One of you bastards came up and bought me a beer. Jesus, that got me. There, right fucking there—love while I suffered. I drank and cried. I drank and talked. I mumbled that Troy was fucking my girl, my Eve.

"Whoa," one of you said. "My granddaughter goes to school with one of yous. Her name is Eve."

"What'd he do to your granddaughter?"

"No, her friend! A little girl."

"What's he doing to children?"

I could have stopped it. Could have stopped all of this. Could have explained. Could have walked away. Instead, I had another beer and let you talk. It was so easy. A raised eyebrow here, a look away there, and with in half an hour you were all convinced that Troy was not just fucking the alligators, but screwing the kids, too. All you wanted was the least excuse, the tiniest hint, that your hate was moral and sweet and good. I gave you that in abundance.

Then I walked back to the farm. I could have gone anywhere and there was only one place I could go.

I thought it'd be quick. You'd come, arrest him, and leave the rest of us to our happy lives. You'd leave me and Fay and Eve 43 and the alligators and everyone. I told you, I warned you, just him.

Now look. You changed our prayers to death chants. Eve 9 chews her tongue and won't sleep. I try to feed her, but she won't eat. You're killing us.

Tonight, before I came here, I went looking for Troy in the woods. I wanted to convince him to give up, to give himself to you. It's freezing tonight. I was shivering fully dressed. And Troy is out in the trees, slinking around naked under that rotting alligator skin.

He found me first, jumped from the shadows and grabbed me by the shoulders.

"Brother. Baby brother," he said. "We all need to die. I know that now. I have a plan. We'll be dead when they come. All of us."

"Troy, they just want you."

He shook his head, said I'd been right the whole time. That you people are evil fucks.

"Troy, I did this." I told him about the bar, about my words and my silence.

He didn't speak for a long time. He looked more dead than the alligator skin. Then he stepped back.

"You don't deserve to suffer with the Family."

I said nothing.

"Go," he said.

"Can I take her with me?" I asked.

He shook his head and turned away.

"Can I say goodbye?"

As he walked back into the swamp, the skin slid off his back.

When it's cold, like tonight, the gators swim to the bottom of the swamp and dig holes. They crawl in and go dormant for the night. But tonight it's going to freeze. They'll come up in the morning and find the surface is ice. And we won't be there to break it for them. They'll drown before it thaws. That's bad enough. But if one gator doesn't get below in time, before the waters freeze, he's left above the ice watching his family drown.

Nobody wants that.

I'll turn off the fence now. You can come in and rescue everyone.

PIERCED

Dear Halley,

 I've done something horrible. Really horrible.

 And right before your wedding night.

 I'd like to blame Rick. Best man, my ass. But it's my fault.

 I've met other virgins, Halley. Plenty. But you're different. You're a virgin by choice. By commitment to a religious ideal that I don't get, but I respect. I still remember the night on your couch and we were kissing and touching and you whispered into my ear, "Let's wait." Those were the two hottest words I have ever heard. I mean that.

 So Thursday night Rick took me out for a kind of bachelor party. Just him and me drunk on four pitchers of some microbrew called Hopalaician Trail. And Rick says, "Lets do something wild!" And I say, "No." And he says, "Oh, the bit's already in the mouth." And I say, "There's no bit." And he says, "Prove it." And I say, "How?" And he says, "Let's do something wild." And I say, "Like what?" And he says, "Prince Albert." And I say, "Fine!" And then I say, "What's a Prince Albert?" And he says, "Too late, you said yes!"

Halley, please, if any love for me remains in your heart, don't google Prince Albert. You won't like it. It's enough to know it's like an earring. On my penis.

I got it from this fierce monster troll-lady. Maybe 4' 11". Stout. Strong. Very strong. She had this hole-puncher thing and she saw my penis and you haven't and I'm so ashamed.

I woke up in the morning and I could tell something was wrong. It should never be this color. Outside of coral reef nature documentaries, I've never even seen this color. It hurt, more and more as the day went on. Like an itch and fever and bruise all in one. This will explain my constant sweating during the rehearsal, why I couldn't stand to hug your father after he gifted us tickets to Hawaii for our honeymoon, and why I vomited a little on your shoe before saying goodnight. It wasn't nerves or cold feet, it was an unclean piece of steel in my penis.

It's only gotten worse. I tried to take it out about an hour ago and almost passed out. My mother came in. I tried to tell her, tried to explain I had done something harmful to myself. She said that everyone felt that way the night before their wedding, but eventually you have children and it's too late anyway.

Oh, it's bad. I'm looking at it now. It looks like a skinhead choking on a dumbbell.

*Halley, I could make it through the ceremony, I
know. I could even limp through the reception. It's only
pain. Then, we'd have the limo and maybe you'd be frisky,
cause you've been waiting, and I'd have to play coy and
I'm not coy, Halley. I am not coy. And the limo would
drop us at the airport because your dad got us tickets to
Hawaii, though I hate the beach, but no one ever asked
me. And then we'd get to security and I'd remove my belt
and the change from my pockets and my shoes and I'd
walk through the detectors and I'd beep. I'd beep, Halley.
And they'd have me step aside, and buzz me with their
metal detector wands while you looked on with that dis-
approving smile I love so much. And the wand would pass
over my crotch and buzz and they'd ask, "What's in the
crotch, sir?" And what can I tell them? And they say, "Sir,
what's in the crotch?" And people are staring and back-
ing away and one of the security guys is unlatching his
gun. "Remove your pants, sir." But I can't show them, not
for my sake, but for your sake. The only thing worse than
having your first penis be a purple, pussy mess is seeing
that purple, pussy mess in public. I refuse. I shake my
head. My mouth dry, his hand on his gun. And the wand
wanders too close and taps the wound and I scream and
grab my crotch. And the gun's pulled. And people scream.
And I scream. And a shot is fired and I'm hit and I fall to
the floor and I see blood pooling from me and I see you,
shoes in hand, stepping back from the blood like a child
from a wave on the beach.*

And then I'm dead.

For you.

And you're left with an urn full of ashes for a hus-band. And when you shake the urn, Halley, it rattles.

I can't do that to you, Halley. I can't. So this is goodbye.

Rick, that bastard, is waiting outside. We're driving to Mexico where I can have this thing removed by some-one who doesn't speak the same language as I do. I don't think I could face someone in English.

Yours truly,
William

P.S. *You'll never see me again. I love you too much for that.*

CHRISTMAS

It was Christmas Eve, almost Christmas morning. He was warm and asleep. She woke him by saying his name, and he opened his eyes to the flicker of candlelight.

"Is the power out again?" he asked.

"No," she said. "Just mood lighting." She was sitting up in bed, smiling at him. The bouncing light filled her face with shadows. Her hair was messed from sleep, but her eyes were awake and excited. "I want to give you your Christmas gift," she said.

"Now?" he sat up and rubbed the back of his neck. She nodded and bit her lip. Her smile was slight. A thin line. All her features were soft and thin. Except her hair. Her hair was long, kinky, and the dark brown of wet soil. He reached his hand into her hair, his fingers working through the thick. Even after two years the texture was wild to him. "Okay," he said, smiling.

She turned away and reached under the bed. His hand fell from her hair to her back. He felt her warm skin through the cotton nightshirt. She faced him again and in her hand was a pistol. She held it flat in her palm, as if she were trying to guess its weight.

"Is that real?" he asked.

She placed the pistol in his palm. He found the gun heavier than he had expected, and colder. She smiled.

"Where did you get this?" he asked.

"It didn't cost much."

"You hate guns."

"It's not loaded," she said. "I want you to do something. I want you to put this in your mouth and pull the trigger."

He snorted a laugh and waited for her to giggle. She bit her lip again.

"Are you joking?" he asked.

"Come on. No big deal," she said. She snatched the gun from his hand and put the barrel in her own mouth. "Shie, no pwobem." She pulled the gun out and laughed.

"Don't fool around."

"It's not loaded." She placed the gun back in his palm. "Do this for me."

"Why?"

"For me."

"That makes no sense," he said, holding out the gun to her. "Come on. Put it away."

She placed her hands under his and closed his fingers around gun. She raised herself to her knees and moved closer to him, lifting his hand slowly, the butt of the gun toward the ceiling. He was having trouble thinking. "Please," she said. He didn't resist her. Even opened his lips a little. He could taste metal. Tasted like lake water. He pulled his head back, away from the barrel like it was something toxic. "Shh," she said. "You're okay." It was the tone she used when he got frustrated with bills, or couldn't fix the heater. It was a sweet tone. Like a mother.

He tried to think. He should stop this. He should want to stop this. He tried putting it all together, lining up all the elements. She wouldn't hurt him, he was sure of that. She also wouldn't put a gun in his mouth. But she was putting a gun in his mouth. His hands on the gun. He was not stopping her. Logic wasn't working.

She took her hands away and he started to remove the gun. "No, no," she said. "Leave it there."

She leaned in and ran her nails along his scalp. The barrel rattled against his teeth. She was close, her breath on his scalp, her dark hair over his eyes, her breasts touching his chest, her smell all over him.

"See?" she whispered. "This is good. You feel close to it all."

Tastes like lake water. That's what he kept thinking. Lake water.

She kissed his neck. "Now," she said into his ear. "I want you to pull the trigger."

His eyes were stinging and his mouth salivating. His throat cramped. He couldn't swallow his spit.

She moved one leg over him, and with a knee on either side, let her weight rest on him. Her face was in front of him. Floating. Blurry. Candlelight slowed to a smear. He couldn't read the numbers on the digital clock behind her. Couldn't remember her middle name. He didn't know her. Hardly knew her.

She put her hands on his cheeks, hands so hot. Her expression was serious now, like a teacher turning stern. "Do this now, or I leave and you will never see me again."

He shook his head and moaned. A line of dribble fell from his lip. She leaned in, "Shhh," and kissed his forehead, leaving her lips on him for a long moment. She leaned back. "This is happening," she said.

Throw the gun. Throw it against the wall, he thought. He could feel the barrel in his mouth, feel his tongue near the hole, feel her heat, her breath, feel his hands on the handle, her legs around his. Could feel each space of flesh, each moving blood cell. It was Christmas in his home, with his wife. It was Christmas and there was lake water and her moving against him. It was Christmas.

HOLY

We have a new holy machine. It will make you a saint. But it will cost everything else. To the world you'll seem two steps north of brain dead. Dribbling and moaning. You'll wear a diaper. But you'll be seeing God the whole time. You just won't be able to tell us about it. No words, no profound acts. Just God. That's what you want, right? Just God. Come on. Let me strap you in.

THE
MARTYRS
OF
MOUNTAIN
PEAK

Kent is dead. All the kids at the camp are crying and singing and praying. They don't know that it was my turn, not his.

Rich is standing in front of us leading the songs. The ten kids who had Kent as a counselor are huddled in the front row. Already seven of them have announced that they've given their lives to Christ—although one is actually regiving his life, since he already gave his life to Christ as a sophomore, but since then he's been smoking pot. None of the kids I counsel have given their lives to Christ, but they look pretty sad.

We're singing "Desperado," but with the words changed. The lyrics are flashed on a screen.

Desperado, why don't you come to love Jesus,
You know that he sees us
For so long now...

It was Kent's favorite song. Pricilla Brone is helping Rich by leading the girl echo parts. She's got tears on her face and her hair is all shiny. She's so pretty it hurts to look at her, especially when she sings. When the song ends, Rich asks us to bow our heads and pray. All two hundred and six teenagers close their eyes and bow their heads, even the kids who hang out at the cigarette pit and usually make fart noises during the prayers.

"God, Father, Daddy—thank you for letting us know Kent. We're going to miss him," Rich says. "But we know that now he's with you and your Son in Heaven. Thank you, Daddy. Amen." People are crying and hugging, just like last week.

"Let me tell you a little bit about where Kent is now," Rich says, his eyes twinkling. He's smiling like a TV dad. Everyone wants Rich to be their dad. He's kind and funny and tells great stories. Better than my dad back home in Houston who's always grumpy and sleeps all weekend.

"Heaven is a lot like Camp Mountain Peak, only better. You can bet Heaven's got horses like we've got. The angels help on the ropes course and the apostles run the four-wheelers and maybe Mary and Martha are scooping Kent a Snack Shack ice cream special right now. I bet Kent is playing disc golf with his halo—oh sure, and they've got a video arcade like us and a thirty-person hot tub like ours and an Olympic-size pool—maybe bigger even, and in Heaven I bet they even have a forty-yard, two-story-high waterslide. Only the one in Heaven won't have a low panel on the curve."

A few kids sob out loud. Kent had been trying to beat the Camp Mountain Peak speed record on the waterslide when he died. According to the slide's digital timer, the record is 23.2 seconds, which I set way back in June. Kent was obsessed with beating it. He was competitive like that, which is totally not the point of Camp Mountain Peak. Rumor has it that when the panel gave he was wearing Speedos and had greased up with baby oil. Total pride. For one thing, counselors aren't allowed to wear Speedos or two-pieces in the swimming area. When I was a camper here five years ago, not even kids could wear Speedos or two-pieces, but they've laxed. And baby oil? I mean, what's Christ-like about baby oil? I was going to die on the ropes course, fully dressed.

"No, the waterslide that Kent is riding right now is faster and wilder than our slide and no chance of falling out, and even if he did, he'd just fall on a cloud instead of down a cliff. You know Kent is just loving that." Kids nod along. Rich crouches down and kind of whispers so all the kids have to lean in to listen. "He's looking down right now on us here and feeling sorry for us. Probably wondering why we're so sad when he's having such a blast. Probably hoping that we're buying a ticket for the Camp Mountain Peak he's at. Only we can't afford that camp. We can't even make a down payment. The price is way out of range. You know why? The price for that camp is perfection. Anyone perfect out there?"

All the kids shake their heads back and forth.

"Didn't think so," Rich says and stands up. "But it's okay because you know who bought the ticket for us? Jesus did. He is perfect and with his own blood Jesus bought us all a pass to the best camp you can imagine, and it doesn't last just two weeks, it lasts forever and ever." He stretches his arms out, trying to show how much forever is.

"And you got to know," Rich says, looking real profound. "The waterslide is the only route from the ledge to the pool, and just like that Jesus is the only path that splashes into Heaven. Nothing else works. Jesus is our waterslide."

I'd heard this several times before, though the part about the waterslide is new. Every two weeks a fresh group of teenagers from all over America comes to Camp Mountain Peak, and every two weeks a counselor dies. It's become an unofficial policy. Always an accident. One of us just acts a little less careful and the rest of us let it happen. It started early in the summer.

The first session was lame. Two hundred or so kids and twenty counselors. We prayed so hard. I remember praying until my head ached, but only one of my kids stood up on the last day to say he had opened his heart to Jesus. Overall only eleven kids stood up. Eleven kids! That sucked. Rich still got weepy and smiley and told the whole camp that the angels were celebrating, so we played "Celebrate" by Kool & the Gang and dropped balloons, but all us counselors were pretty bummed.

Session two was feeling a lot like session one. The kids loved the four-wheelers, the theme parties, the hot tub, the rappelling lessons, but didn't give a spit about the Lord and Savior. They were too busy making out behind the dining hall to care about God bearing the burden of their sin. I had this one kid from Denver in my cabin who said that his hobbies were "pounding beer and pounding babes." I caught him having sex with a girl in the hot tub after hours. I told him that every time he puts his penis in a girl who's not his wife he's putting a nail into Christ. But he still didn't give a squat.

Then on the last day of the session, Will died. Will was a counselor who also took care of the horses and he was practicing a stunt for the Farewell BBQ and Hoedown when he got thrown. It was horrible. Like someone punched the whole camp in the stomach. We went ahead with the BBQ and Hoedown, but it was no fun.

That night, standing in front of all the kids, Rich looked tired and sadder than I've ever seen him. "You know what, I don't feel much like talking tonight. But you know what? Will would want me to tell you about Jesus." Rich didn't move on the stage or crouch or whisper or spread his arms at all that night. Just stood in the center and talked. "That's what he'd want. Because, yeah, we've got some fun stuff up here, we sing some fun songs and the ribs tonight were pretty excellent, but the only reason, the only, only reason, is so we can tell you about Jesus. And Will would gladly die if it meant that just one of you would have a chance to meet Jesus."

I mean, kids were falling over themselves to give their lives to Christ. One hundred and ninety-seven kids stood up and told everyone how they now love Jesus. And the ones who didn't stand up felt pretty stupid and probably came to Christ on the bus ride home. Even my hot tub kid from Denver stood up, all crying. He told me he was never going to pound a girl again.

"Except your wife," I said, and we laughed. I gave him his own *Adventure Life New Testament* and hugged him goodbye. That was the best.

After the kids left and before the next group rolled in, we counselors started talking. Rich was right. It was worth dying to see kids loving Jesus. We stayed up real late in the Coffee House, just the counselors, praying and singing and reading *Acts* aloud. And it was like the Spirit was leading us. There were four more sessions in the summer so we drew lots like the disciples did to replace Judas. I got session six, the last session of the summer. All the counselors were crying and smiling. They laid hands on the five of us and prayed. Pricilla Brone had her hands on me. They were warm. I was so happy, so filled with the spirit, so ready. I could hardly wait till my session. It was like promising to die made God more real. I could touch God. I was scared, sure. But Jesus was scared. He cried in the garden. I was scared like he was. At dawn we all climbed to Christ's Point and sang hymns.

After that we never spoke of the agreement, not letting our left hand know about the right hand. In fact, by the middle of session three, I was beginning to think nothing would actually happen, but then Crick Peppers "accidentally" locked herself in the kitchen freezer. In session four David Blankins "forgot" to open any of the garage windows while doing repairs on an idling four-wheeler. Becky Towt choked on a doughnut in session five. I have no idea how she managed that. My plan had been to "forget" to strap in on the ropes course on day ten of session six, but then Kent had to go and slip out of the waterslide and fall off a cliff.

The kids I counsel are all somber as we walk back to the cabin.

"He must have been going damn fast to fly out like that," one of the kids says.

"I heard he shaved his legs to make him slicker," another says.

25

"Man, he was brave."

I pray for these kids a lot. Every morning I wake up before Morning Bell and pray God will crack their hearts open like walnuts. I love them. How can you not love someone you're planning to die for? I used to imagine them all crying after I died on the ropes course, sorry they hadn't listened or gotten to know me. I pictured them standing up on that last day and telling everyone they love Jesus and then coming back to Mountain Peak years later with their kids or grandkids and pointing out the spot I died at and holding hands with their grandkids and everybody praying and thanking God for me.

I tell them to head back to the cabin and I'll be there in a minute. I don't have to worry about them sneaking out. Nobody sneaks out after a death.

I go walking toward the ropes course.

The stars are amazing up here. The camp is dark. They turn off a bunch of lights when things are sad so the kids can see the stars, especially the shooting stars. So many stars, and Jesus made them all. He knows them all by heart. He knows every single hair on my head. He knows I'm walking now, he is right here with me. But I can't think of anything to say, cause I'm kind of mad. God knew about that low panel. He knew about the baby oil. He knew it was my turn, but he let Kent put on those Speedos and shave his legs and fall out.

At the Buenas Vista View I stop and look out over the valley. It's windy, a little chilly, but I don't care. It was at this spot I opened up my heart to Jesus five years ago. I didn't need a dead counselor. I just heard all about the Father's love and my sin and how they whipped Jesus with this nasty whip with glass in it and then Rich said that if we wanted to have some time alone we could go off and I walked out here and I prayed for a sign and God sent a shooting star right over Camp Mountain Peak. It was wild. Like God ripping the sky just for me. It turns out that you can see like three or four shooting stars every five minutes, but still. I've come back every summer since then. I was a camper twice and a junior counselor twice, then last year Rich made me a full counselor. This place is more home than home. It's my favorite place in the universe.

I walk on to the ropes course. It's spooky at night, all the trees and ropes making shadows. It's real dark too. Smells like pine needles and bark. I think I'm alone but then I see Pricilla sitting on the observation deck, dangling her legs. I go and sit by her and for a while neither of us says anything. Finally she says, real quiet, "So I guess you won't be dying then, huh?"

"I guess not," I say. Her hand kind of touches mine, just the fingers. A wind comes by and a few leaves float down.

"So, you want to pray?" she asks.

"Sure," I say. We bow our heads and our faces kind of get close, real close, touching and…I don't know. We just start making out. Like totally making out, tongues going all over the place and hands under clothes and yeah, Jesus sees, but I'm like, yeah, look at this Jesus, this is a tit, Jesus, and my hand is on it. And she's touching my hair and my arms and my legs and between my legs and it's like praying but faster and more heat and she's touching my zipper and I'm touching her zipper and there might be a billion shooting stars but I don't care. Then Rich shows up with his flashlight and catches us. Pricilla starts buttoning up real fast and I'm trying to hide the bulge in my jeans.

"Sweet Jesus," Rich says.

I'm staring at the wall in Rich's office. He has a picture of every summer staff since 1970 and above them a wooden plaque that says, "The harvest is rich but the workers are few."

Rich isn't saying anything yet. He's just rubbing his eyes. He already talked to Pricilla. I waited outside. I heard her crying. Rich looks real tired.

"You know the rules, I know you do."

I nod. My throat feels full, like it's packed with wet sand.

"You left your kids unattended. They were worried, you know. They came and found me. I was worried. Then I find you and Pricilla. On a day like this, too."

I try and say something but I can't talk.

"I'm sending you home, okay. I'm sending you home tomorrow and I don't think you should come back next summer."

I think I'm going to bawl, I mean just wail. But I don't. I get cold.

I walk back to the cabin. A couple of kids are sitting on the porch. They don't look me in the face when I tell them to hit the sack. They just mumble and stay where they are. I walk inside and lie down on my bunk.

I can still hear them talking on the porch, but I can't tell what they're saying. I lay awake for an hour or two till everyone is sleeping and breathing heavy. The cabin smells like cedar and sweaty laundry. I've always loved the smell. It smells safe. But now the smell makes me feel ashamed. Everything does. Shame like a real hard blush, like a blush that's going to stain my skin. Then I think about Pricilla and her hands and I immediately pop a woody, then a lot more shame. So to stop the woody I think about my mother. Then I think about Kent's mother. She sent that care package with the Rice Krispies treats. When I close my eyes I see Kent. He's at the bottom of the cliff all bent up and in his Speedos and there's no blood, but his skin looks funny and you can tell he's dead. Bastard. So I imagine myself down there instead. I imagine the falling and the landing and the cracking. Then the woody starts to come back, which is weird, so I get up and go out on the porch.

I look out on the dining hall, the volleyball/basketball court, the crafts store, saying little goodbyes to everything. I see a few kids sitting in the cigarette pit. It's way past curfew, almost morning, so I head over there to tell them to go back to their cabins, and they all look a little green, a little fuzzy, even their cigarette smoke is green and fuzzy. I recognize Will first. Then David and Crick, and Becky and last of all, Kent, still in his Speedos, still smelling like chlorine and baby oil. All just standing around, smoking. Sitting behind them, lighting one cigarette from the end of another is Jesus. He looks totally different than in the movies, shorter, kind of dirty, but you can tell it's him. You just know.

"Hey, guys," I say, and I'm breathing fast. They don't look at me. Just sit and smoke.

Kent says, without looking up, "Turns out we're wrong about the whole Jesus thing."

"What do you mean?"

"Jesus doesn't save," Becky says, still sounding like she's got a doughnut in her throat.

"He doesn't?" I look over at Jesus, who just shrugs.

"Maybe Buddha does," Crick says. "Or Shiva."

"My money's on Zoroaster," Becky says.

"I've never even heard of Zoroaster."

"Narrow is the way," Jesus says with a shake of his head and a chuckle. "Want a smoke?"

Oh God, Jesus is talking to me. Looking at me. Jesus is asking if I want a cigarette. This is everything. Jesus is hanging out with all these guys, awarding their devotion, like he hung out with Peter and John and James, making them fish for breakfast.

"Can I stay here?" I ask. "Can I stay with you guys?"

"You got to be fucking kidding me," Kent says.

"You…" I point at Kent. Sitting there all smug and bruised, just a few feet from Jesus. "You stole my place, Kent. That's my place."

"You want it? Come and take it."

I run at him. He doesn't move, just takes another drag on his cigarette. I slam into him, only it's more slamming through him and for a second my stomach drops and knots, like I'm standing on the edge of a canyon. Below me are miles of nothing. Then I'm past him and I smack into a pole.

When I open my eyes I see Jesus. He's looking down at me, and he looks sad. Disappointed, I guess. Me trying to fight Kent's ghost, me and Pricilla. All these thoughts I'm not supposed to have. He died for me and this is how I thank him?

"Jesus," I say, "I'm sorry."

He looks so sad.

"Jesus, please forgive me."

He smiles. His teeth are black. "No," he says.

"I have to ride that fucking waterslide a hundred times a day," Kent mumbles. "Ungrateful bastard. A hundred times a day."

As he's speaking the clouds begin to go pink and their green bodies start fading.

"Jesus?" I say, getting to my feet. But Jesus is making eyes at Becky. "Jesus!" They fade away as he scoots over to light her cigarette. The green flame is the last I see of them.

I'm still standing there when Rich comes out of his office, same clothes as the night before and his eyes red like he hasn't slept a wink.

"Grab your stuff. We're leaving in five minutes."

Pricilla and I sit in the back of the camp van as Rich maneuvers the windy road with the mountain slanting up on one side and cutting down on the other. As we pass the sign that says GO WITH GOD, Pricilla starts to weep a little. I take her hand.

"I had a dream about Kent," she whispers. "He was smiling and flying. He had this white robe and was so happy." She smiles. "And we were singing, him and me. We were singing 'Jesus Loves Me.'"

I think of telling her about green Jesus and the smoking and the canyon feeling inside Kent. But why? It won't make her happier. Doesn't make me happier. And maybe it never happened. Maybe I dreamt it all. And Jesus is just as he has always been. Loving me. Watching over me. Maybe this is real faith, believing when you know it's not true.

Rich's head bobs to the side just a little as she and I start softly singing.

"Jesus loves us, this we know…"

I see Rich's head bow and I think he's praying. Then the van drifts and hits some small pines on the side of the road. Rich jerks up and pulls on the wheel and we're skidding. Pricilla squeezes my hand. A wheel catches the edge and the van tilts so hard I hit the ceiling. Through the windshield I can the see the valley and the trees and some sky, and we're falling and turning and we're floating inside the van, like the inside of Kent. Just before we hit, I swear I hear Pricilla whimper, "Save us Zoroaster."

TONIGHT
AT
NOON

Mingus is no good for hangovers. You want something softer. Bill Evans or Chet Baker. But I like Mingus, even if he hurts my head, so I flip on the stereo and let him play.

It's noon. Already hot, sunlight sneering through the blinds. Jenny's not in bed. She's always up before me. On the speaker by the door, there's a roach bouncing to the music. I've got to get more roach bait, though Jenny hates the stuff. She hates roaches too but thinks the bait boxes are cruel tricks, unfair fighting.

There's a smell in the hallway. A bad smell. Like the toilet's backed up.

I find her in the kitchen. She's naked and on the floor. Eyes open. I fall down beside her and say her name. I shake her. I check her pulse, but I know. Her skin feels like damp rubber. Not quite cold, but not alive. My knees are wet. I gag. I don't yell. She has a piece of paper taped to her belly.

> **Don't tell anyone what I did. Tell them I went to Mexico. Love Jenny**

I look around the kitchen for the cordless phone. I don't see it. I run into the living room.

I find the phone on the receiver. There's a note taped to it as well.

> **Please**

I put the phone down and walk back to Jenny.

> **Don't tell anyone what I did. Tell them I went to Mexico. Love Jenny**

Jenny left the comma out after *Love*, so it's not so much a signing off as a command. *Love Jenny*. I laugh. Then I feel sick.

She's small. Long fair hair that she'd forget to wash. The note is taped to the pooch under her belly.

No blood. Maybe there's a mouthful of bleach missing from under the sink. Maybe there's an empty bottle of sleeping pills in the trash. Maybe something else happened. Was she alive when I went to sleep?

I sit on the floor and look at her. My hand hurts because I'm biting it.

I get up, close the blinds, pull the curtains, and make sure the doors are locked. Then I sit and watch her some more. Mingus is still playing.

She looks wrong on the kitchen floor.

I towel her dry and sit her on the couch. She's stiff and smells. Not like rot. It's a different smell. It's the smell under the bleachy smell in hospitals. She looks better on the couch. More comfortable. I try to cross her legs. Her legs used to be so ticklish. Just a touch and she'd start kicking and squealing.

"I'm going to peeeeeee," she'd say.

She's wearing that leather wristband I got her on South Congress. Just a leather strap, like a belt for her wrist. Seventy dollars. Seventy dollars, but she just had to have it. That was Jenny. Just HAD to have it. Just HAD to do it. As if nothing was a choice, all things were inescapable. Just HAD to die.

I should cry and yell. I don't feel like crying. Her corpse is on the couch looking at me. Mingus is still playing. It's *Mingus Ah Um*. Maybe his best. Most people say *The Black Saint and the Sinner Lady* is his best, and it's good. But *Ah Um* is going for more. It hurts more. Lives more. Jenny is dead.

I need coffee. That will help me think. A slow cup. I make enough for two out of habit. Jenny likes hers Miles Davis black. I add milk to mine until it passes Coltrane. Then some honey to get the color of Mingus. Almost yellow. Name a race and Mingus had the blood. Black, white, Indian, Chinese. A Klan man's treasure chest. Kill half a dozen races with one rope.

I place the cups down on the coffee table and sit across from her.

Jenny had been with me for three months. Ninety-two days. She moved in a week after I met her. She came over one night and never left. I liked watching nature documentaries with her, liked the way she made the sheets smell, liked drinking Lone Star on the porch with her, liked how she rubbed my neck with her chin, liked how she bit my nipples at odd times like breakfast. I loved taking care of her.

"What would you do if I died?" she once asked.

"I don't know," I said. "Cry, I guess."

"But what would you do with the body?"

"Nothing."

"Come on. Let's say you found me and I was still warm."

"That's sick."

"Not for two consenting adults. Don't be such a prude."

"I'd call 911," I said.

"So they could rush me to the morgue before I got deader?"

"Why do you keep asking?"

"Do you love me?" she asked.

"I just met you."

"Do you love me?"

"Yes," I said.

"I'm going to ask for a favor."

She was alive when I went to sleep. I'm almost sure. I sip my coffee.

When I was nine a friend told me that a scorpion would rather kill itself than touch fire. I didn't believe him. "Animals don't do suicide," I told him. We got a can of lighter fluid from his garage, trapped a scorpion under a paper cup and made a foot-wide circle of lighter fluid around it. We lit the circle and lifted the cup. The scorpion snapped its claws at the fire, scurried to one side, scurried to the other, returned to the center and in quick jabs, bent its tale and stung its back over and over. Its body twitched a little, then went stiff as the flames died out.

"See," my friend smirked. "I told you."

Jenny loved this story.

"That sting always hovering," she'd say, "like holding a gun to your temple twenty-four hours a day."

"What was worse," I told her, "was the beetle we put in. No stinger. No choice but to wait for the fire. It freaked out, running in circles. I was about to reach in and grab it out when my friend squirted a line of lighter fluid from the circle straight to the beetle. It kept running while it sizzled up. Its shell cracked in the fire."

"Jesus," she said.

"I never told anyone about that," I told her.

She shrugged. "Some things are sins only if people know."

I think she's smiling. Sitting on the couch and smiling at me. Just slightly. Almost a sarcastic smile. And she doesn't want me to tell.

Bury her? Maybe. But where?

Drop her in the lake. No. They'd find her.

Take her camping and leave her for the birds.

Boil her flesh, feed the soup to the neighborhood cats, use the bones to make a wind chime.

Take her to Mexico in the trunk of my car.

She's waxy. Her skin and her eyes. I guess the eyes go first, all water and all. I put Jenny in her pajamas. She usually sleeps in the nude, but she looks cold. Jenny would do this thing with her toes. While we were making love, which she liked to do often, she'd wrap her legs around my back and tickle my ass with her toes. It made me tense up and more than once ejaculate immediately.

She laughed all the time. She wore these long cotton skirts and she'd run through the house laughing, pulling off her shirt and pushing down her undies—that's how she let me know she was in the mood—but she left the skirt on. She liked that, the feeling of the cloth being pushed up, bunching around her thighs.

Sometimes during lovemaking we'd put on music. Monk or Davis. Maybe Coltrane. She didn't like Mingus. "It's too much. Too many notes," she'd say.

"Coltrane's got a bunch of notes."

"Different. Those are less planned. Mingus' music is like a whacked out prophet screaming about the end times. Babble babble babble. But saying something."

"There's no babble, if you listen."

"But I don't want to really listen. I want to concentrate on you."

"Now you know how the toe feels."

It must be around four in the afternoon. I pick her up from the couch and carry her into the bedroom. Her body doesn't want to bend and she's heavier. I have to be careful walking through the bedroom door.

"Carry me across the threshold," she'd once said. "Like we're married."

I put her on the bed, tuck her in. Pulling the sheets to her shoulders, letting her feet stick out at the bottom of the bed. That's how she likes it.

Mingus claimed he had banged twenty-three different women in one night. It was in a Mexican whorehouse. He said he just went wild. Couldn't stop. One after another, after another, after another. If I go twice in one night, I'm a hero.

I lay down next to her. Smell her new smell. I bet her insides are turning to liquid.

"Do you ever just hurt?" she once said. "I mean for no reason. Or all reasons, in a way. Life just hurts. Even beauty hurts. And worse, I can't get behind it. I know something's there, but I can't get to it."

"That's what Mingus has been trying to say."

"Fuck Mingus. Fuck him up his Mingus ass."

"Jenny!"

"Don't you ever feel a lonely so deep the whole world couldn't help? And it doesn't help that others feel the same thing. Doesn't mean anything. In fact I hate them for trivializing my thing, my loneliness."

"Your thing? Loneliness is not your thing."

"See? You're doing it. I'm trying to tell you, it is mine. But I can't tell you anything without using these fucking words."

"Someone's feeling sorry for herself."

"Fuck off."

"Jenny!"

"Fuuuuck off."

"Okay, I'm going to sit outside and let you calm down a little."

"While you're out I'm going to drink all the rubbing alcohol."

"Don't make a mess."

"I'm going to drop the toaster in the bath."

"We don't have a toaster."

"The hairdryer then."

The sun is setting behind the blinds. Still hot. I'm beside her. I sleep for a while. But not well. I think I feel her kick. I hear her fart. Hard to sleep with her here.

Mingus froze up. That's how he died. His arms and legs stopped working, his whole body died, but he was too stubborn to leave. Like the landlord turned off the heat and electricity to try and force the tenant to move out.

I get out of bed and flip the light switch. There's a roach on the pillow by Jenny's head. It's staring at me. Kind of twitching at me. Jenny would hate this.

We had this one roach living in the bathroom drain. You'd see it anytime you took a middle of the night piss. We called him Larry. He was fast. We hated him, but with a kind of affection. One night Jenny yelled for me.

"Larry's moving all slow. He looks sick."

"Must be the bait," I said.

"Just catch him and take him outside. Let him live in the wild." She smiled.

"No, I'm going smack it," I said. "It's already dying."

"I thought you loved animals."

"Roaches don't count."

"That's like saying Jews don't count as humans."

"It's nothing like saying Jews don't count."

Then she cried. I had thought the conversation was all easy. Just funny. But she went to bed weepy. I smacked Larry with an *Entertainment Weekly* and flushed his remains. Then I drank a beer on the porch. When I did go to bed there was a note on my pillow:

> **Just for that I'm sending my whole family**
> **to lay eggs in your shoes.**
>> **Love, The late Larry.**
>> **Formerly of the Sink**

Jenny opened her eyes and giggled as I read the note. I giggled too. But my feet itched for a week.

"Larry?" I ask the roach on Jenny's head. It twitches. It moves on to her forehead and looks at me again. I keep waiting for Jenny to brush it away. It crawls over an eye. Come on, Jenny, brush it away. It's on her lip. Twitching. Near her teeth.

"Fuck off, Larry!"

It speeds up the wall and is gone.

I go to the kitchen and find a black roach bait box in the trashcan. It's been cut open and I can see the food. A beige, sweet smelling paste. Looks like marzipan. There's not much left of it. How much does it take?

The coffee is cold, but I drink it.

I smell rot. Sick rot. Sad. Jenny hated the idea of growing old. Not of being old. She liked to think of herself being really old, a strange aged thing hobbling around town with a funny hat and a tendency to yell. But in between here and there freaked her out. She still had a decade before forty, but she was already noticing her body drop. She wanted to freeze it young until slam-bam she was ancient. No in between. But even death couldn't stop her growing old, breaking down, wrinkling up. Process. Can't stop it. Like running downhill, too fast, throwing your legs in front of you hoping you don't fly head over heels. No control and no chance of gaining control. Like Mingus in some session, playing so fast, losing it, finding it, playing around a note, not on it, around and around and around till the note is clear because it's the one thing not being played. Melody in reverse.

I draw a bath for Jenny. Steamy water with lavender aromatherapy. I put a shower cap on her and prop her arms over the side. The arms don't dangle, they stick out, palms down. I wet a white hand towel and fold it over her eyes. She looks fine.

"Shower over a bath ten to one," she had said. "Showers move. A bath is standing still. You can feel a bath cooling the moment you get in. A shower keeps giving hot. More hot all the time."

"Unless you're second in line and your girlfriend takes half-hour showers," I said.

"It's still moving. I'd rather have cold water moving than hot water sitting."

But she looks good in the bath, laying still. "Not so bad, is it?" I say. Then I give her some privacy.

In the bedroom I put three Mingus CDs on shuffle. "Haitian Fight Song" starts and I move with it. Tempo keeps jumping, so I'm jumping. One speed, another speed. Hopping and jumping, dancing like I'm the stand up bass, sometimes popping, sometimes swaying, sometimes going faster than I can think. Eyes closed and sweating. And his notes are touching the melody in places it didn't know it had, making it bend out of itself. And you can feel the melody's pleasure. Hear her moan. Then comes "Slop," "Passions of a Woman Loved," "Blue Cee," "Gunslinging Bird," and then "Tonight at Noon"…fucking madness, that song. Horns like horses being slaughtered, and another horn hypnotizing a snake. The bass riff like an oversized spider goose-stepping in fast motion. The piano being stomped on, danced on. And behind it all Mingus is screaming. Then comes the drums, machine guns into a circus parade. Everything screaming. Everything dying. Everything moving.

I fall on the bed. I close my eyes. I want to eat it all up. Gobble it down. Gobble her until there's nothing left. Tell everyone she's in Mexico, while all the time she's in me. Too late now. Too far gone. Couldn't salt the rot out of her.

My shirt sticks to my skin. My hair sticks to my head.

I go to collect Jenny, but she's not in the tub. She's gone. But I'm wrong. She's there, just under the water. Must have fallen. Maybe my jumping jarred her. The white towel is floating, so is her hair. My first thought is to grab her, yank her back into the air. But I stop. 'She's dead,' I tell myself. 'Stop trying to save her.' The surface is still. She must have been under for a while. I lean over and look at her, and my fingers touch the water. It's cold. Maybe I could freeze the water, freeze her in a tub of ice. Thaw her out right along with Walt Disney. She looks pretty under the water. Blurry behind the soap. An air bubble slips from her nose and rises toward me. It shocks me. I grab her with both arms and pull her up. 'She's dead,' I tell myself and I stroke back her hair from her face.

"I can hold my breath for six minutes," she'd said.

"No you can't. No one can."

"I can. I used to do it all the time. You just got to not think about breathing."

"That can't be good for you."

"No worse than smoking."

"You don't smoke," I said.

"So I can afford to hold my breath."

"Why do either?"

"Shit," she said. "You've got to do something."

I towel her off and dress her in her favorite blue dress. The crinkly one. I sit her on the couch again. Her skin is loose. That bothers me. And I can still smell her under the lavender. I sit across from her. The smile is growing. A sliver of teeth is showing. I close my eyes and take some deep breaths. Try and slow it down. Try and slow it all down.

It's dark outside. Night. Later we can leave. Maybe drive away. She just smiles.

I turn out all the lights. First in the living room, then the kitchen and bedroom. All of them, till the whole house is black. Jenny loved this game. Hide and Seek in the dark. The seeker tries to make the others give themselves away. Make them snicker, then you find them.

"Jenny?"

I walk from the bedroom slowly. Hands out in front, feeling walls and doors in the darkness. Carpet to tile. So quiet. Just my feet on the tile and the refrigerator humming. Part of me doesn't want to make a noise. Just wants to hide in the quiet. But that's not how you play.

"Jenny."

The idea is to make them laugh.

"Jenny, Larry is upset that you ate his bait. He'd grown to like it."

I touch the couch arms.

"Jenny?"

There's a hiss. An exhale. I step back. Legs hitting the coffee table. Reach for the lamp. I turn it on with a twist, but send it falling with the same motion. For a moment I see Jenny and her smile. Then the smash and the room is darker than before.

"Jenny?"

I take a step and trip on the lamp. I crawl. Hands on wood, plank by plank. My hands touch something small, smooth. The roach bate. I hold it hard, the torn edges cutting. Crawl. I touch feet.

"Jenny?"

Climb to her knees. Crawl up, on to the couch, beside her.

"Jenny?"

I take her hand. My other still holding the bait. I squeeze her hand.

I don't move. I don't breathe. In the room black changes to different shades of dark. Outlines and objects. I wouldn't move. I wouldn't breathe. Jenny, I wouldn't even breathe. I don't want to die, Jenny. For no good reason, I don't want to die. And even if I did, I don't think I could. Stop squeezing, Jenny. You're hurting my hand. Let's just sit here in the dark. My heart is popping like a stand up bass, Jenny. We'll just sit here and listen to my heart. Just be still. In a few hours we'll leave. I'll put you in the car and drive you to Mexico, okay? The sun will be up by then and it will burn all the black away. Okay, Jenny? Okay?

CHALLENGING, REPULSIVE, AND AWESOME

Did you find everything you needed?
Good.
Diet Coke, Twix, Camel Lights. I'm surprised you smoke. Your
teeth are so pretty.
More gum. Already? You bought some this morning.
I remember. You came in this morning. Last night, twice. Four
times yesterday and three times the day before, once at three
AM. That's a lot of Stop&Shop.

I understand. It seems like I'm always here, right? Like I never
leave? Well, it's true. I am always here. I never leave. I'm the
only employee of the 24 hour Stop&Shop.

Really. First I was hired by a tall man originally from Nigeria. I don't know who hired him. Someone who lives somewhere else.

I was made night manager in December. I called my father to tell him. He was in a nursing home and didn't understand any more. It didn't mean much, night manager, just that I worked nights, ten to six. At six in the morning the tall man from Nigeria came in for his shift. One day he didn't. I waited, but nothing. And the customers kept walking in—morning rush for coffee and energy bars. So I served.

The afternoon woman came in at two and I went home to sleep. But I couldn't sleep. I fed my cat and sat on my couch and waited for eight PM and the Stop&Shop. It was growing then, the idea. So simple. Great ideas are simple, like Slim Jims. I worked that night and by morning I was hoping, maybe praying, the Nigerian wouldn't show. But he did. So I fired him. I fired him with a strong voice claiming authority from someone who lives somewhere else. And the Nigerian left and didn't come back.

For four months my life was two shifts and an empty third. My father died in his sleep.

One day the afternoon woman came in crying. I told her she could go, I'd cover her shift. My first consecutive twenty-four hours in the Stop&Shop. Sometimes you see the change your life can be. You see it right before you. When the afternoon woman came in again the next day I handed her five hundred dollars and told her to find a good man.

Then it was just me. That was half a year ago.

I lost the apartment, I'm sure. I'm sure they raised voices and taped warnings to my door.

I think about my cat—I liked the cat. But the cat never liked me. It only came for food and water. That's all gone.

Stop paying rent. No home.
Stop feeding the cat. No cat.
These are the bonds we build a life on.

But you see, I am doing something here. You smile, but listen.

This used to be a job. My hours had a price tag and it was small. I was as bad as the cat that stayed for food. Now I burn my paychecks in a metal trashcan. All my needs are met. Slim Jims and powdered-sugar donuts and sugar-free Rockstar Energy Drink. I eat in the quiet hours. When I'm alone and the ice machine hums.

Sleep? No, not really. I don't lie down, that would be inappropriate.

I used to take quick naps behind the counter. But that was silly. Shameful.

With discipline, the mind can do amazing things. Don't smile. Really. Let me explain.

My father owned a book, *The Oxford Dictionary of Saints*. He loved the saints. Do you know St. Simeon the Stylite? He was a pillar hermit. He lived on the top of a forty-foot-high column in the middle of a city for thirty-seven years straight. Had a platform up there, about the size of this countertop.

They called him holy. Bishops and emperors visited him. They'd yell up questions to him—bishops and emperors! And at Lent, just to make it harder, he would spend weeks without sitting or lying down. Just standing up there, praying. This is real. Documented history. The book said he "provided a spectacle at once challenging, repulsive, and awesome."

And I know how he did it.

Like sleep. I've split my head in two and allow one half of my brain to sleep while the other half works. I'm getting so good at it that some of the regulars think I'm two twin brothers running the store. One brother is logical, no nonsense, good with numbers. The other brother is dazed, but friendlier and kind of artsy. He gives back the wrong change but in beautiful designs, little silver constellations of nickels and dimes in your palm.

I'm touching your hand. That's probably inappropriate.

I should tell you, I am peeing right now. It's okay. I am wearing an adult diaper, aisle two. Still, it takes a certain amount of effort. I try not to leave the store unattended. I do not go outside. Ever. That's why my skin looks bad. But what's skin compared to all this?

Why? It's not clear?

Well, if my left brain were on duty, I would simply point to the OPEN 24 HOURS sign and inform you that I am the sole employee. My right brain might answer with some poetic quip, like, "May my reason be free of reason. Fa la la." But the both brain truth of it is: "Challenging, repulsive, and awesome." How could you want more than that? And know, you must know, Simeon didn't live on a column because he was a saint. He became a saint up there, somewhere along the way.

My cat had been my father's before he went to the nursing home. He always had a cat. One would die and he'd replace it with a new one. We can't go out, he'd say, the cat needs to be fed. Can't play music too loud—the cat. Can't travel. Must work. Must feed the cat. He thought his life meant something because he fed a cat.

Hush.

Cats feed themselves.

You—you are unnecessary to your own life.

I—I'm doing something. I'm doing something here. Something challenging, repulsive, and awesome.

You laugh, but I could smell the mediocrity of your life as soon as you passed through the automatic doors. It's stinking up my store. You work some job you don't like, holding your breath for eight hours a day. You spend your free time on eating, TV, and sleep, or looking for someone to eat with, watch TV with, and sleep with. But I don't sleep. I'm awake. Your soul is as soft and pasty as my skin. But my soul is as sharp and cool as the silver caps on your rotting teeth.

Sorry. Sorry.

Not appropriate.

But you will keep coming back. You will keep checking, seeing if I'm still here. You'll try odd hours, and you will always find me. You will ask me math questions and my favorite colors trying to discern which half is at the helm. Some days you won't talk. Every now and then you'll buy something, a Slim Jim, perhaps, or a sugar-free Rockstar Energy Drink. You will linger. A little longer each visit. You'll eye the adult diapers. Your skin will change like mine. You will forget to go home. Forget *how* to go home. Finally, you will come to me and ask for an application for employment, maybe a stocking job in the back. And I will give you one. Because we're always open. Always.

Here is your change. Here is your purchase. Thank you for shopping with us. Come again.

LICORICE: A STORY FOR JOHN ERLER[1]

Zane Bellows: a natural pop star sensation. He was six feet tall with hair that spiked up like flames from a grease fire. He could reach his lanky arm up through the branches of musical composition and pluck the ripest, sweetest little tune, the kind of melody that you'd hear and think, "Why wasn't that written before?" He'd add some reasonably inspired lyrics and find himself with another hit, songs like "Fruit Fly in Your Eye" and "I'm Stoned and Voting."

But in the fall of 1986, Zane Bellows outdid himself. He and his band the Sea Elephants began recording *Licorice*, the

---

1 If you're not John Erler, please don't be discouraged. Perhaps I've missed the spot trying to write a story for John Erler and hit splat damn on a story for you. If this is John Erler . . . hi.

most ambitious album of rock history.[2] In a time of pop and plastic, the band set out to create starlight and ambrosia.

It began with pain.

Zane Bellows broke his toe on Lane Rope's mislaid bass as the band's tour bus barreled through Austin, Texas. The pain burst from the toe up the leg like oil from an old-fashioned oil drill.

The emergency room's younger nurses squealed when they saw Zane draped between Polk and Shelly Wallenhump, lead guitar. The older nurses had Zane replace his leather jacket and pants with a short gown that felt and looked like paper towels.

One nurse gave him a generous dose of Vicodin and left him in a quiet room to recoup. The neat little narcotic started in his head and slowly floated downward, like those thick fogs he'd left in San Francisco, hiding the pain as it went, down his neck, sinking into his stomach, descending along his leg and welling up in the toe. It didn't stop the pain as much as covered it and made it less important.

Zane was always an explorer, always restless to see what was around the corner. He was alone for fewer than ten minutes before leaving his bed and heading into the clean smelling halls, his bare feet slapping against the cool floor, his happy ass smiling sideways at anyone caring to look.

While walking, Zane glimpsed into the rooms of other patients. He saw cancer, dying hearts, and broken bones. He tried to magnify the pain of his toe so he could relate to the pain of these others. Vicodin was working against him. He couldn't quite empathize, but he wanted to.

---

2 Though knowing you and your passion for Brian Wilson, I'm sure you'd argue that *The Beach Boys' Smile* gives it a run for its money... not the 2004 or 2011 version, but the one we never heard.

Through one of those windows, Zane Bellows saw a woman. She was tall, almost Zane's height. She had slouching shoulders and a thin waist. A bright blue top loosely curtained her chest and a lime colored skirt rested on her hips.

Her hair was straight and brown, the shade of oak-bark, and she had ghost white skin that was covered with a light white fuzz. Her eyes were gray-blue and sad. She stood at the foot of a hospital bed, studying a young man lying there. He was still, his eyes closed, tubes in his arms.

Zane felt protected from the sorrow in that room only by the door—like looking into a radiation chamber, knowing that if you open the door even a crack all that radiation would zip out and scar your eyes, throat, and skin.

He might have moved on, considering the danger of a leak, but Zane remained a moment too long, and the girl, sensing his stare, turned and smiled. From straight on her eyes had an even deeper sadness, which made the smile all the more startling.[3]

Zane forgot about his toe. He forgot about the Sea Elephants. He forgot about music. He remembered the first time he tasted chocolate. Zane Bellows opened the door.

She introduced herself as Stella.[4]

"I'm Zane Bellows," he said. No reaction. She hadn't heard of him and Zane, much to his own surprise, was glad. They spoke quietly. Simple questions, simple answers. Just sounds exchanged more than words.

After a long while, Zane asked who the young man in the bed was.

---

3 You once said to me that a man must love and serve a woman because woman has suffered so much. That's one of the reasons you loved her.
4 Yes, that's right, just like the name a young Marlon Brando propelled from the depths of his soul at the end of the film. She's heard it before. Don't do it. Zane didn't and she was pleased.

"David, my fiancé."

"Oh."

Oh, that *oh*. Such an *oh*. Like the *oh* collectively sighed by the population of Pompeii as the volcano's innards streaked the sky. The *oh* Captain Smith murmured as he counted the lifeboats on the sinking *Titanic*. The *oh* gasped by the pilot of the Enola Gay as he glanced in his B29's rearview mirror and saw the bright white and reds devouring Hiroshima.

"What's wrong with him?" he asked.

"Coma. It's been seven months now." Stella brushed some of the dark curls from David's forehead and, for the first time, Zane noticed the small diamond ring she wore on her left hand.

Zane Bellows was released from the hospital that same day. But for the next week, he returned to the same room each and every day. He told the other members of the band that the rest of the tour would have to be canceled since he had been ordered to the hospital daily for physical therapy.

"For the toe?" Polk asked him.

"For the toe," Zane replied.

But each day he spent talking with Stella. She would sit on one side of the bed, Zane on the other, and sparks flew over David's prostrate figure like cars on a high-speed overpass. With eager ears she listened as Zane babbled about art, life, the smell of chlorine, or anything else that popped from his buzzing mind. After seven months of conversation with a comatose man, Stella was happy to listen. Her eyebrows, also white, would rise at the subtleties of Zane's humor. Even her breathing matched the rhythm of his speech.

Zane adored her breathing. He was fascinated with the movement of her generous chest and the shudder of her thin lips, but most of all it was the smell. A rich smell like the soil of a rose garden. The breath, wafting from the other side of the bed, soaked right through Zane's person and assured him that he was in love as much as the smell of roast beef would assure him he was hungry.

Then on Zane's fourth visit, Stella stood up and excused herself to the little girls' room and the smell remained. At first he thought, "Ah, her breath lingers." But then it lingered longer than expected. And it never diluted. Minutes passed and Zane slowly realized that Stella could not possibly be the source of the sent that had seduced him so. His eyes fell to the only other breathing being in the room: David. David, as pale and still as the statue who shared his name. His hair as curly and his features as noble. David. Hadn't Zane always been pleasantly aware of his silent presence? Hadn't Zane aimed at least part of his storytelling in his direction? Wasn't it true that Zane never once asked, never once desired, to see Stella outside of this room, away from David?[5]

Zane watched David's slow breathing. He leaned in closer and caught the warm breath spiraling up like smoke from a chimney. He imagined tracing the breath backward, past the chapped lips, the unmoving tongue, the long red larynx, the spongy lungs, muscle, pumping blood. Stella returned and Zane quickly stood up, cracked his knuckles and said he had to be going. Her wide eyes questioned, but she only said, "Goodbye."

He walked the streets of Austin until late into the night, and then continued walking into early morning, drifting in a

---

5 You're not gay. You are homoerotic. I would say you believe in the erotic in variety of forms. But people who know you could see you as gay. I think this turns girls on.

confused downpour of thought. It was not just that he, a confi-
dent and accomplished heterosexual, found himself drawn to a
comatose man. Not just that he also found himself attracted to
the young woman this same man was engaged to. What squeezed
Zane's mind was that he loved them both, as a unit. He loved Stella and David, David and Stella, her open eyes and his faint breath.

As the dawn sky blushed over Austin, Zane surrendered
all preconceptions and was born anew. "I love them both," he
muttered to the sun. "All things can be."

Zane skipped back to the hospital, giggling as he went.
He waved at bakers opening their stores and laughed at bank-
ers and businessmen streaming into tall, glass buildings.[6]

At the hospital he was told that visiting hours were from
3 PM to 6 PM.

"Don't worry," he told the aging nurse behind the desk.
"I'll be back." She assured him that she would not worry, and
Zane bolted.

Later that morning, Zane booked a studio on South Congress. It was a large space with hardwood floors and black, egg
crate walls. He gathered the band and announced a new project entitled *Licorice*.

"Why *Licorice*?" Shelly asked.

"Because licorice can only be described with the word
licorice," he explained. "Bite into it and you have no idea what
it really is, but it is definitely licorice."

They started recording that day.

Zane's heart-altering experiences drove him to attempt
the new. He wielded the microphone as if it were a supernatu-
ral sponge. He carried it outside to record the afternoon sun.

---

6 You've been in love. "Goofy love," you called it.

He placed it to his and the other band member's foreheads to soak up emotions.

For that first day's vocal sessions he asked that the entire band and the sound engineer be in the nude.

"Can I keep my boxers on?" asked Lane Rope.

"Yes, of course," Zane answered. "But each and every thread of fabric will find its way onto this album and bear witness to your shame."

Lane Rope removed his boxers.

At 3 PM Zane was sitting with Stella/David in their tiny, white room.

"How did he get like this?" Zane asked.

"Slipped, hit his head on a doorstop," she said with a sigh. "Completely random."

The concept of random chance became an integral part of the recording process. During one session, Zane released a bag of moths into the studio to interfere with the playing. He hid alarm clocks throughout the studio, all set to ring out at haphazard intervals. On another track Zane had the band switch up instruments so that the bassist was on drums and the drummer had a guitar and the guitarist was on vocals.

The rest of the band felt lost. The new directions were disorienting. Imagine playing a game of pool on a deep-sea fishing boat. If you're concerned with the rules of the game or even the rules of land-bound physics, the act would be utterly frustrating, but if you forget about how the game should work or how the balls should roll and just enjoy the colliding of multicolored spheres as they bounce about, popping in and out of pockets, well, then you'll have a blast. But the band just wanted to play pool.

Zane tried to inspire them. He told them all things are possible. He predicted that *Licorice* would end the Cold War.

"It's just an album," Lane Rope said.

"Nothing is just anything," Zane shouted. "Anything is everything."

But they didn't understand. In frustration, Zane would retreat to David/Stella. His unmoving strength. Her sweet, soft glances. His stoic resolve. Her sighs and eyes. They were Zane's muse, his magic, his door into more.[7]

"What did David do with his time before the doorstop?" he asked one drizzly winter afternoon.

"We own a gag gift store. You know, fake poop and things." Stella reached into her purse and pulled out an oversized nickel and handed it to Zane. It looked exactly like a nickel, except it was four inches wide.

"That's funny," Zane said, and he and Stella laughed.

"David designed that."

Zane patted David's chest. "Very funny."

Laughter became another key element of the *Licorice* recordings. Zane used laughter as an instrument, hiding giggles in the mix or featuring a snicker as a solo. Zane recorded the laughter of dozens of people of all ages, all ranks, all different levels of joy. The tenth track on the album was seventeen minutes of laughter overlapping and combining.[8]

---

7 You and I were once watching a blue jeans commercial in which a couple faces a herd of buffalo plowing toward them. They take each other's hands and the buffalo stream all around, but leave the couple unharmed. "That's what it feels like to be in love," you said. "You feel like as long you've got the other you can do anything." A cliché, certainly, but such a passionate cliché.

8 You're enthralled by laughter in music. I'm sure your passion is inspired by Brian Wilson. As I write this I'm listening to you on the radio (KUT). You've been playing songs with laughter in them for much of the morning. Laughter: rhythmic, repetitious, melodic. Isn't laughter where music began?

Zane wanted to include Stella/David in the recording process, so he often used their gag gifts to inspire the laughter he recorded. Once while walking to the studio for an evening session, Zane was asked by some tough looking street kids for a little change. Zane pulled out the oversized nickel and told them, "All I have is big change." The kids beat him severely. Zane hurried on to the studio and recorded himself laughing with a fat lip. The flapping of the lip made for a wild bass sound on track six. Lane Rope was jealous.

But the other Sea Elephants were starting to follow Zane's lead. Shelly suggested recording at least one song in complete darkness and it was Polk's idea to fill a microphone with catnip and let a stray kitten provide the percussions for track four.

Zane had announced to Polygram that the new album would be complete by spring and it would be extraordinary. Already the rumors were churning. Greedy record executives rubbed their sweaty little hands and set the release date for the week of Easter.

Zane Bellows was changing more than only musically. He donated his leather pants to Goodwill. He took less time in the mornings to sculpt his hair. He smiled more.[9]

"Do you think David is happy?" Zane asked on winter's afternoon.

"I don't think I've ever seen him happier," Stella said.

"Are you happy?"

"Yes," she said.

---

9 Remember how change snuck into your life? It was because of her. You hardly knew it was happening, but one day you found yourself kinder.

She wasn't. Stella was a tortured soul. She had grown fever-ishly in love with Zane. And accompanying that love was a yappy runt of a dog named Shame—shame for her unfaithful thoughts in the very presence of her betrothed. Quickly following and sniff-ing the ass of Shame was an even nastier mutt: Resentment. Un-like Zane, she could not conceive of a balance between the three of them. She began to hate David for standing (or lying) between her and Zane. Soon Stella was spending sleepless nights being chased around her mind by a savage pack of mangy mongrels.[10]

Those same sleepless nights, Zane sat in the studio alone, remixing, changing, splicing, adding harmonies and atmo-spheric twists, often venturing into bizarre regions of sound and rhythm where even the other Sea Elephants couldn't fol-low. When Lane Rope discovered that Zane had backtracked his bass line on track nine and used it to accompany the sounds of dolphins making love, the bassist confronted Zane.

"Can't we just record some normal songs?"

"We're trying to transform the world here," Zane said from his seat at the mixing board.

"I'm a bassist. I have no interest in transforming any-thing." Lane Rope said. He collected his gear and left. Zane didn't bat an eye. He just returned to the mixing.

By Valentine's Day the album had only to be mixed and mastered. Zane was nearing exhaustion, but he managed to bring David/Stella a dozen red roses and a book on the Holy Trinity. Three was holy to him now. David as Dreamer. Stella as Listener. Zane as Creator.[11] Stella smiled at the gift. Zane was

---

10 Part of me wanted you two to fall apart. I'm sorry, but you were almost offensively happy. Watching that kind of love can be stressful. But then you cried, and you're not the kind to cry. Lots of days you wouldn't answer the phone.

11 I had thought you were not in this story. None of the characters are based on you. But perhaps you are here. Perhaps the three (Zane, Stella, and David) are you. Zane is action; David is inaction; Stella orbits the two like a comet between stars. Is your genius your contradictions? Is your being the unlikely love affair and hate affair of anonymous elements? The pain and joy of your year has pushed out the edges of your soul. In some ways it can hold more than it ever held. But the seams are torn and your soul pours out on me and all those you see.

too preoccupied with telling her about the finishing touches he was putting on *Licorice* to notice that Stella was no longer wearing her engagement ring.

Over the next month Zane worked almost without ceasing on the album. Occasionally Shelly or Polk would drop by, but for the most part, Zane worked alone. Then on March 14, just minutes before midnight, *Licorice* was completed. Zane made a master tape and rushed to his most precious audience.

He bounced up the stairs of the hospital and down the hall to the room where David lived. Before he opened the door, he glanced through the window. To Zane's surprise, Stella was there as well. She was whispering into David's ear. When Zane walked in she looked a little shocked, but smiled.

"I'm so glad you're both here," Zane said, his face glowing. "I want you both to be the first to hear *Licorice.*"

Stella said nothing, just nodded and watched as Zane readied a tape deck and turned off the overhead fluorescent lights so that the only light came from the door's window. Zane pressed play. He took his seat on the other side of the bed and the music began.[12]

Colors heard, sounds tasted, secrets shared. Moments as subtle as whispers, others wailing out. There were smells in the songs, the scent of sex and rain and even David's breath. Lyrics simple as a child's nursery rhyme and filled with riddles and stories.

Zane swayed, his eyes closed, his hands waving. Stella watched him in the dim light and her eyes began to melt. The melodies tugged on her until she arched across the bed and

---

12 You loved her when she danced with you riding piggyback, stumbling, laughing, making love to *Smiley Smile.*

put her face close to Zane's. She placed her lips lightly on his. Her hands were on the bed, just touching David's hip. Zane's eyes were still closed and to him it was as if the music were touching his lips. He gave into the softness. Floating notes, floating flesh, and he let his hands fall onto David's stomach and pelvis.

Below them, the sheets began to rise. Zane and Stella's hands crept closer to each other, and closer to the peak between them. The final song of *Licorice* began a crescendo climb. The notes—higher and louder. The growing—taller and firmer. The hands—closer and closer and touching. Zane heard a perfect note he had not written, a sound he had not recorded. He heard the sound through his ears, through his lips, and through his fingers. It shimmered and echoed like a note struck from a triangle. It was a gasp, a breathing. Zane opened his eyes. In front of him was Stella, her lips still wet. Below him was David, eyes wide. Zane was surprised to discover they were blue. He had imagined them as brown.[13]

The last sustaining moments of *Licorice* hung in the air, the three were wide-awake and together. David blinked at Stella and then at Zane.

"Stella," David said. "Did I miss the wedding?"

The song ended.

"Oh David," Stella held his head to her breast.

Zane tried to smile, tried to look at David, but he found the way David moved his mouth grotesque. And his voice, it was squeaky.

The hidden track on *Licorice*, Zane's favorite track, burst from the tape deck.

---

13 Maybe you love her even more now that she's gone.

"What is that noise?" David asked.

"Noise?" Zane whispered.

"Zane, will you turn that off?" Stella said, her eyes never leaving David's.

Zane pressed stop. He watched Stella cradling David, and David reaching to touch her face. Stella's small diamond ring fell from David's open palm, hit the floor, and rolled to the tip of Zane's foot. Zane reached down and picked it up.

"You dropped this," he said.

Stella said nothing, just squeezed David's head to her chest.

Zane placed the ring down, quietly collected the tape, and walked from the room. He made his way down the white hall, yanking the black tape and letting it trail behind him.

The next day Polk arrived at the studio to discover the *Licorice* recordings were nowhere to be found. Polk was convinced some other band had snuck in and stolen the recordings, but then he found a single tape with a note saying, "Goodbye." The tape had just one song, Zane on guitar and vocals.

Over the next few weeks the band was too shocked by the disappearance of their album and friend to do anything. But after a month and plenty of pressure from the record label, Polk added drums to that one remaining song. Shelby gave it a guitar solo and harmonies. They called in Lane Rope to lay down a bass line. Finally the song was released as the last single of Zane Bellows and the Sea Elephants.

The song was so happy, a bubbly bubble-gum nugget, like vanilla Coke and Girl Scout cookies.

You know I love to feel the beat. Dead ahead is loving street.
Music kills my blues. I'm never all alone now!
Are you alone now?
Are you alone now?
Are you alone now?
Baby, I'm coming on over.

It was a huge hit. Billions sold all over the world. The Sea Elephants (sans Zane) went on tour based on its success alone and all retired as wealthy individuals. It was a sugary, sticky piece of pop candy glory.

But if you listened to the words—not every word, only every third word—the song is one of the saddest pieces of music ever recorded.

~~You know~~ **I** ~~love to~~ **feel** ~~the beat~~. **Dead** ~~ahead is~~ **loving** ~~street~~.
~~Music~~ **kills** ~~my blues~~. **I'm** ~~never all~~ **alone** ~~now~~!
~~Are~~ **you** ~~alone now~~?
Are ~~you alone~~ **now?**
~~Are you~~ **alone** ~~now~~?
~~Baby,~~ **I'm** ~~coming on~~ **over**.

What happened to Zane Bellows? Some say he and *Licorice* sank to the bottom of Town Lake. Some believe he didn't destroy *Licorice* at all and is simply waiting until the world is worthy of hearing it. Still others claim he's in India searching for the source of all sound.

The truth is, Zane Bellows changed his name and his appearance and began a career as a freelance jingle writer. You've heard his work. His songs have sold everything from dog food to diapers. But in each lighthearted jingle Zane slips subversive hints and harmonies, like hiding hallucinogenic mushrooms in Wonder Bread. Once again change is sneaking in. Zane Bellows is transforming the world one commercial at a time.[14]

---

14 *I'll take the dream that you and I and junior and all our friends old and new and all the good people in the world are gonna live lives of total ecstasy and one by one slip into Heaven where there'll be Gladys Knight records and licorice for all.*
　　　　　　　　　　　　　　　　—Abbie Hoffman, in a letter to his wife.

THE
ADVENTURES
OF
STIMP

Stimp was trying to get the key to turn on his apartment door. It was getting dark and he was frightened.

"You're all right, you're all right," he whispered to himself, trying to twist the key. But he didn't believe he was all right.

Stimp could hear Pumpkin squeak from inside the apartment. Pumpkin was a hamster, a fat hamster. Some days Stimp could hardly see her eyes for the fat and fur surrounding her face. She was so brave. Never afraid. Sometimes she'd crawl to the top of the water bottle and jump over to the wheel and get her fat little legs caught in the spokes. She smelled like hamster. A wheaty, wood-chippy smell. The whole one-room apartment smelled like hamster. Stimp smelled like hamster. He couldn't smell it himself, but he had overheard someone at the post office mention "the aroma of gerbils." The person had said, "gerbils," but Stimp knew he had meant hamster. So Stimp had made an effort to not smell like hamster. He had washed, purchased special perfume-enhanced soaps, stuffed his pockets with potpourri. He had even given Pumpkin a very unappreciated bath. But you can't get the smell of hamster off a hamster any more than you can get the smell of baby off a baby. Now babies, that's a smell. Stimp liked that smell, but he was afraid of babies. He had once held a baby, his mother's neighbor's baby. He hadn't hurt the baby, but he had imagined what it would be like if he had. Like if the baby just wriggled a little too much, or some loud noise made Stimp throw his arms up in the air like he'd done with that platter of Ritz Cracker sandwiches at his mother's housewarming party. Crackers hit the ceiling, some stuck there. Which is bad for a cracker, but really bad for a baby. And they probably wouldn't believe it was an accident. They'd probably think he wanted to hurt the baby—not just hurt, those crackers splattered—kill the baby. The judge would be all stern and say something like, "Let the hamster-smelling man with the tiny, crooked penis approach the bench." But how did the judge know about his penis? But Stimp wouldn't ask because that would be contempt. His lawyer was no help. A cheap, state-employed lawyer who wouldn't like Stimp. He's all, "I'll prove my client is innocent," but winking at the jury and whispering under his breath, "Innocent of showering, ha ha." And they all laugh, which is nice for them, because they're all mad at having to be a jury instead of at home or at work. No, instead they have to watch a child-killing, cracker-smashing, hamster-smelling, small-crooked-penis-having, gerbil-fearing, scabies-suffering guy on trial. And who would take care of Pumpkin? Probably no one. Pumpkin could be starving in her cage, especially since he had put the brick on the top so that she wouldn't get out. But now he wanted her to get out. To get free! Not to have to eat her own leg or something. Hopefully she'd try around the water bottle. The mesh is loose there. Yeah, and just in time because here comes Mr. Crawnan, the world's worst landlord. Knowing Mr. Crawnan, he wouldn't even wait for the trial to end, he'd go right ahead and rent the place and sell all Stimp's stuff, which is totally illegal, not that Stimp can talk, since he killed a baby. Except his vinyl collection, Mr. Crawnan would keep that for himself. He had once even said, when fixing a lightbulb, "Nice album collection." Yeah, right. Nice. You mean *very* nice, as in very nice for your love nest upstairs with all its purple pillows, felt walls, and mood lighting. Yeah.

So he'd be stomping, Mr. Crawnan that is, all around the apartment, clumsily searching for the albums, which are hidden. Stimp would hide them for sure. Note: first thing tomorrow, hide albums from Mr. Crawnan. And while searching he smashes the Precious Moments figurines, which is okay cause they're creepy and Stimp only kept them because his mother gave them to him, but he made them face the wall cause their eyes are all big and freaky. And Mr. Crawnan knocks over the hamster cage just as Pumpkin nibbles through the mesh around the water bottle and Pumpkin jumps into her clear plastic ball, rolls out the door, down the stairs, and into the stream just behind the apartment building. And Pumpkin doesn't care a tinker-tat about the fish staring at her through the plastic because she's coming for Stimp, her friend, so Pumpkin gets to the prison where Stimp is because Stimp lost the trial, and she sneaks Stimp a key, pretending just to be a mouse. Stimp's cellmate, Rocko, doesn't tell on him cause he has become such a good friend cause he had scabies once, too. And he understands how Stimp feels being oppressed because of the small, crooked penis. Not because Rocko has a small or crooked penis, his penis is fine. But Rocko is black and black people get oppressed, which Stimp understands because he owns three Ray Parker Jr. albums, so Rocko wishes Stimp luck as he sneaks out, but Rocko stays cause he's trying to get his GED. And there's a huge search for Stimp, but Pumpkin leads him to a safe place to hide. A circus, where Stimp guesses people's middle names, only it's a scam because they have to show their driver's license to get in the circus and the guy who sees their license tells Stimp their middle name through a radio in his ear, but sometimes it's just an initial and Stimp has to guess and he guesses wrong, but the circus boss says that's okay cause it makes it look more real, and say, don't I know your face, say, I hadn't noticed the smell because of the elephants, but say, aren't you the Hamster Man that killed that baby? And Stimp has to run and hide in the woods where Pumpkin teaches him how to live as one of the beasts. Free. Alive. Strong. But when the winter comes, there are no more berries or leaves or anything and even Pumpkin looks skinny. Pumpkin scratches a picture in the dirt showing a stick figure man eating a stick figure hamster and Pumpkin crouches by the drawing and nods her little head and points her little claw at her little chest and Stimp is so hungry he almost does eat Pumpkin, but instead he cuts off his own pinky with a sharp rock and makes a tiny fire to roast it over. He feeds most of it to Pumpkin and saves just a morsel for himself. As the months go by he takes another finger and another and another, till finally he only has one finger left and he can't hold the sharp rock, not even with his toes, which would have been smarter to eat first, but now he and Pumpkin just lay on their backs, hoping it will rain in their mouths, but it doesn't and they die. Which is sad because Rocko, now out of jail and a captain with the police, is looking everywhere to find Stimp and when he finally does, he sees Pumpkin and Stimp both dead, Pumpkin cradled in Stimp's one remaining finger. Rocko cries and tells the dead Stimp he was innocent because the baby was already dead when it was handed to him and the mother knew it, and she just wanted to blame it on Stimp so she had given him the baby and had paid someone to make the loud noise, so it's okay he threw the baby, and that he broke out of jail, and he has a strange penis, and he smells funny, and he's always afraid, and the key turned and the door opened and little Pumpkin squeaked to see Stimp home. Stimp closed the door behind him and sighed. "No nibbling. Good hamster."

Then he put on his favorite Ray Parker Jr. album and they danced. Stimp jumping and flaying, Pumpkin rolling back and forth in her plastic ball.

FOUR
TINY
TALES
CONCERNING
TRANSFORMATION

1
The Yellow Stone

I sit and mindlessly dig my fingernails into the thin tree bark, peeling it away and letting it fall to the mud. I like the smell.

As I dig, I find, smack dab in the middle of the tree, a tiny, yellow stone. Like a jewel, sort of, I think at least. I have never seen a real jewel. Plastic stuff, well, yes. Mother did enjoy her collection. Tacky I suppose, the collection that is, but my yes, they were tacky times.

So I begin to pick at the yellow stone, thinking of wealth and my mother. It's wedged in, but I'm determined to get it out. I'm not lacking strength. I once dated a tennis player. Strong, very fit.

As I pick away, sweating and grinding my not-so-false teeth, I groan. Groans of stubborn desire, well so I thought, but I begin to sense that the groans are more ones of pain.

Then I make another realization.

I wasn't the one groaning.

I stop in mid-pick.

I listen…I listen again. I skip the third listening and move straight on to my fourth listen.

Could the groan be coming from my yellow gem?

No wait, just wait (and a fifth listening).

Is the gem moaning? Or worse, is it the tree? Have I discovered that trees do indeed feel pain? Please no, a hard salt-encrusted *No*. If trees feel? Years of pulp and paper screaming at me for past crimes. Writing, reading, bottom cleaning. No. Not the tree, I couldn't live with the guilt. It would be too much. Far too much. Like beets on a salad.

What then? I poke at the bark. What would this be? Then, wonder of wonders, a section of the wood, incredibly similar to the shape of a small lizard, transforms into a golden purple. And my stone seems in a timpth of time to be bedded in a purple pillow of this lizard shape's head, with a newly appearing counterpart. A twin, if you will, only a space away.

"Well, well, well, well," said I. "What is this?"

To my surprise (though probably not to your surprise, you smug little bastard) the lizard spoke up.

"See here," the voice began. "I am a creature of skin change." His accent seemed to be German, or Chinese. Same thing in its fullest. "I am a chameleon, a rather rare wood-dwelling chameleon, and you, fair digger, have not only destroyed my summer home but also waged war against my eye."

"I saw only a stone."

"Yes, a stone. A false eye. I lost my real one some years ago in a boating accident. So now I have this glass clump instead. Because of its foreign origin it remains unchanged as my color blends."

"Yes, well. Sorry." I did feel bad. Imagine. But he's the one who put it in the tree.

"I have filled my wound," he says, slowly crawling higher up the tree. "And will never fully blend in again."

2
Don't Tell

- Don't Tell
- Look, don't tell anyone this happened.
- Of course not.
- Because I'm not like you. This was a one-time thing.
- I understand
- But, well, it was nice.

3
The Turtle and the Snail
~ A bedtime story ~

One day Mr. Turtle and Mr. Snail slowly slumped along the shaded forest path, conversing, cajoling and singing happy songs.

Happy is good.

Mr. Snail turned to Mr. Turtle. "Isn't it a wonderful day?" said Mr. Snail.

Of course happy isn't everything, some things like heroin or certain women make you happy, but rot your heart. Heart rot.

As they were talking, two speckled bunnies streaked down the forest path, hopping and giggling.

"Hello slow-pokes," said one bunny laughing cruelly while leaping from side to side of the turtle and the snail. "You should leave your heavy homes and come run with us."

"But the shells are our protection. Our special talent," said Mr. Turtle.

"Have it your way, slow-jokes. Ha!" said the other bunny and off the two bounced faster than running water. But not faster than a shallow woman's appetite for something new. That's for damn sure.

Mr. Snail began to weep. Which is dangerous for a snail, because tears have salt. Burning tears. Tears burrowing into skin and soul. Those kind of tears. But you wouldn't know tears. No. No time for tears. Too busy snuggling with your new Math Professor boyfriend—wooing him with your child-sized tennis shorts and a Joe's Crab Shack neon tank top.

"I just wish I was speedy-speedy as the bunny," said the sad little snail. "Or pretty-pretty like the butterfly. Or smarty-smarty like the fox. There's nothing special about me."

"You're my friend," said Mr. Turtle. "You're special to me."

"Thanks, Mr. Turtle," said Mr. Snail with a slow smile. "But the bunnies are so mean."

"Don't let them get you down," said the wise and happy turtle. "It's not like a woman you trusted and cared for dropped you flat on your ass after two and a half months of love-giving. Heaps of love-giving. When she was hurting, you were there for her. You even loaned her money, which she never paid back, not that you want it. You don't want it, although it would pay for the Pink Floyd CD she never put back in its case so it's too scratched to play anymore because she never had respect for anything that wasn't hers, fucking selfish soul-ripper, Mr. Snail. So take it easy, Mr. Snail. You're fine just being you, Mr. Snail."

"I'm tired of being me," Mr. Snail said. And without another word he slipped from his shell.

"You look like a slug," said Mr. Turtle.

"But I move like a sparrow." And with that Mr. Snail darted down the path. Of course Mr. Snail still couldn't slink that fast, but compared to his previous speed with his shell-home, he was really moving. "Goodbye, Mr. Turtle," Mr. Snail yelled, leaving Mr. Turtle in slimy cloud of dust.

Mr. Snail was having a wonderful time rushing past trees and stones. The forest was an exciting blur. "Weee," he squealed. He had never felt so free, so alive. That's when he came upon the corpses. Two speckled bunnies, their soft fur shredded and their eyes wide and glassy.

Mr. Snail heard flapping wings pounding above. He looked up to see a dark brown hawk with a blood stained beak hovering above him. Sound familiar? Hawk. Beautiful at a distance. Deadly cruel when close. Then off to new prey. Heart-eater!

"If only I had my protective shell," thought Mr. Snail. "I could hide and be safe. But I've exposed my soft, sensitive self and now that bitch of a hawk is going to eat my heart." He let out a tiny, frightened sob. The hawk turned its head, drawn by the chance to cause pain, and stared at the naked snail.

"Caaw Caaw," cried the hawk.

"Crap," squeaked the snail.

The hawk swooped down, moving like wind. Mr. Snail tried to scamper, tried to scurry, but could only squirm slowly away. He could feel the flapping fury just behind him and knew any moment he would feel the snap of the hawk's beak. But then, just before him, appeared Mr. Turtle. And did you know I know Mr. Math Professor? That's right. In fact, I'm having lunch with him today. Did you know I know about your secret shoebox? The one you keep in the panties hamper. I wonder if Mr. Mathy would like to know what's inside the magic shoebox? I doubt you've told him. I doubt you've told anyone ever. Or how about some other little secrets. Diary entry, April 5, 1987? How do you think he'd like knowing about that? Who's exposed now?

"Into my shell, Mr. Snail," Mr. Turtle said. Mr. Snail dove as best he could into the shell and Mr. Turtle pulled in his own head and legs. The hawk, unable to slow its dive, smacked into the rock hard shell and fell unconscious onto the forest floor.

"Thank you, Mr. Turtle," said Mr. Snail, fitting himself back into his own shell.

"What are friends for?" said Mr. Turtle. Then the two tied the hawk to a stone and feasted on its body, devouring the bird piece by piece, slowly. Its pitiful hawk cries filled the forest until Mr. Turtle snipped off its tongue with his snapping jaws.

Sleep tight.

4

Everyone Else

Remember the man who used to work the smoothie shop? He's dead now. Remember the librarian, the one with the big tooth?

Dead. Remember that one kid who got held back in third grade because he kept crapping his pants? He's pretty sick. He'll be dead soon.

I guess that's everyone.

LORD

BAXTOR

BALLSINGTON

Stanley adored being alone with his penis. Especially in the morning. Stanley was laying awake in the early stillness that always followed his wife's departures. She had woken an hour before, hurriedly dressed, and left for her law firm. Stanley was currently unemployed.

Stanley yawned and smiled, his eyes still closed. Trickles of gold light dripped through the curtains, but the room was dim enough and the curtains thick enough to keep Stanley separated from the oncoming day. He let his hand wander.

"Hello," he said to his penis.

Stanley rolled back the sheet and there stood his friend, proudly surveying his realm. As a child, Stanley had christened him Baxtor. Later he added the last name, Ballsington. Most recently he had granted Baxtor a royal title. It was now Lord Baxtor Ballsington.

"I'm sorry I kept you waiting," Stanley whispered.

"Never worry," Lord Baxtor Ballsington said, his voice deep and stately.

"You're a king, Lord Baxtor."

"No, no."

"She was late leaving today," Stanley said. "Maybe we should have done it when she was in the shower."

"You are naughty," Lord Baxtor said, nodding.

"But now we have all day."

Stanley wrapped his palm about Lord Baxtor Ballsington and indulged. The process was lacking in creative verve, but there was more than enough enthusiasm. Stanley didn't fantasize. He didn't need to. He was right where he wanted to be. Pleasure, rhythm, and soon a mounting pressure, a building tension, like a tottering on the edge of a cliff, franticly waving arms, don't fall, do fall, don't, do, too late to stop now—that's when his wife opened the door. Stanley yelped, Paula screamed, Baxtor did what Baxtor does.

Paula closed the door again. Stanley curled into a ball. Baxtor cowered away.

"It's natural," Stanley said a few minutes later, kneeling in a bathrobe before his wife. She sat on the couch, her face in her hands.

"It is not natural," she looked up. Her eyes were red and teary. "You're married."

Stanley dropped his head.

"I need some coffee," his wife said, standing from the couch.

"Aren't you going to be late for work?"

"Work? Fat chance. I can't go to work in this state, with the image of you defiling our bed in my mind."

Paula was a lawyer with the firm Chills and Grey. She loved it. She adored the cool, clean halls, the hardwood floors of her office, the windows with their six story view, her large oak desk where Melissa, her office assistant, would place coffee or a Red Bull while Paula spoke on the phone, laughing at jokes only lawyers would understand.

"So I told him, he might as well file for a 438 as hope for an opposition being granted." And they laughed.

But it was always a somber laughter, the laughter of the trenches. She knew the intimacy of battle, the rush of the fight, the rich smell of others in fear. And beside her, like a squire, was her office assistant Melissa. Always there to supply a file or a fax, a Red Bull or an encouraging grin.

Today was casual Friday at Chills and Grey. The employees could wear whatever weekend-esque clothes they desired. Melissa looked best in her casual attire. Sometimes she even wore shorts. Long legs. There was something intriguing about Melissa's thighs. It was those thighs that had encouraged Paula to take on the Hot Springs Low Carbohydrates Diet. Soon, she imagined, her thighs would be as slender as her trusty squire's. Sometimes she wished she could look a little closer at those thighs, in an academic sense.

"I can only say sorry so many times, Paula," Stanley said, standing in the doorway of the kitchen.

"I want you to promise that you will never do that again." She was watching the coffee drip drip drip.

"Never?" He said. She spun around.

"Yes, Stanley, never," she said. "Is that too much to ask?"

In truth it was, but Stanley just shook his head. Baxtor grunted.

"What was that?"

"Nothing," Stanley said. "I'm going to take a shower."

"No funny stuff."

In the shower Baxtor just hung there, letting the water dribble off his deflated form.

"Baxtor, I had to promise," Stanley pleaded. "Don't give me that look. Come on."

"No, no. Don't concern yourself with me. No."

Stanley and Paula had had sex a total of three times in the last eight months. None of these instances had been much of a success. The last truly enjoyable bout between the couple had been their second wedding anniversary last spring. That was nice. Sweet. Warm. Paula had been drunk. Drinking was an essential part of foreplay for Paula.

A week after their anniversary Paula had begun the Hot Springs Low Carbohydrates Diet. No alcohol at all. Sex became a blue moon event.

Stanley now suspected that he had grown to prefer masturbation to lovemaking. More than once during his infrequent marital duties he found himself fantasizing that his wife were not below him and instead he was alone with Lord Baxtor. He found it amusing, and a little disturbing, that as a teenager he had often pleasured himself while imaging he was making love to a woman, and, now, as an adult, he made love to a woman while imaging he was pleasuring himself.

"Don't pout, Baxtor."

"Please, don't give me a second thought."

Paula was sipping the coffee. It was incredibly strong. She could hear the shower running, but there was not enough hot water in the world to clean Stanley. Not if he was scrubbed down. Not if a thousand nurses with sponges and soap helped. Nurses scrubbing with hot, steaming water till their little uniforms were all soaked through, all wet, all soapy. She better call Melissa.

"I'm sorry, I won't be in today. My husband is sick." The truth of the statement almost had Paula smiling.

"No problem, Mrs. Poppen," replied the toasty voice of Melissa. Paula missed toast.

"Could you cancel my one o'clock for me? And we still need that fax from district, Melissa."

"Yes, Mrs. Poppen."

"Okay, then," Paula said. "I guess I'll see you later then."

"Yes, Mrs. Poppen."

"So, Melissa, what are you wearing?"

"Excuse me?'

"For casual day, today. I'm just curious, you know, not being there and all." There was a knot in Paula's stomach.

"Um, I'm wearing some baggy blue jeans and a sweatshirt, that one with the rabbits on it."

Paula felt strangely relieved.

"But later I'm going jogging, so I brought my shorts."

Oh, God, Paula's legs twitched. "Where will you change?" Paula asked.

"Oh, I guess, maybe your office, since no one's here."

Paula grabbed the kitchen counter. She heard the shower turn off.

"Okay then, just remember that district file, goodbye." Paula took a gulp of her coffee and set to preparing herself some bacon. No toast. No juice. Just bacon. Paula enjoyed the strict regulations of the diet. She found the discipline invigorating.

Paula had grown up in a non-believing Baptist family. They had relinquished all the comforts of faith, but retained the restrictions. They didn't go to church, but they didn't go dancing either. One of the reasons she had allowed herself to be wooed by Stanley was that he threatened none of her "morals." Not out of morality, but out of dullness. A dull man is often a moral man.

The afternoon was tense. Stanley did some yard work. Paula shuffled papers. Neither said much of anything to the other.

She watched through a window as Stanley raked dead leaves. Did she love him? She would say yes. But only because the word *love* has no clear definition. *Love* is not a word used to describe facts. As a lawyer, Paula simultaneously enjoyed and feared the ambiguity of such words. In a law case they could be a help or a hindrance, depending on how they were used. But they were never certain. Never stone. Like Stanley himself, these vague terms served a purpose, but it would be foolish to build a case on them.

Paula stood in the kitchen nibbling on beef jerky. This house bored her. This man. This body. She wanted a potato. She was restless.

"I'm going to the office. I'll be back by dinner."

"She's gone," Lord Baxtor observed from Stanley's shorts.

"I gave my word."

"I wasn't suggesting anything. Just remarking on the fact that she is not here."

"It doesn't matter where she is." The rake rumpled the leaves. "A promise is a promise."

"Oh, of course. Like 'I promise to have and to hold.' But you haven't had her or held her in quite some time. So you turn to me. I imagine she's found release as well."

"Paula would never touch herself."

"I didn't say that."

"What are you implying?"

"Had to run off to the office, did she? Back by dinner? I imagine she'll have developed a ravenous appetite."

Paula sped toward downtown as the sun set behind her, painting the waters of Lady Bird Lake. The first of the post-work joggers circled the lake with bouncing strides. Soon Melissa would be joining them. Probably just now changing in Paula's office, removing her tight blue denim and slipping her long legs into her scanty red shorts. Lean on the desk to support yourself. You're all alone in there. All alone in your boss's office. Who's naughty? Who's a naughty one? Paula accelerated. She decided not to call ahead. No need. She'll walk right in. It's her office. Yes, it is, you naughty girl.

By the time she had arrived, most of the lawyers had left for the day and her footsteps echoed through the quiet lobby. The elevator lumbered up slowly. Paula tried to calm herself by humming along to the Muzak, but when the doors finally opened to the sixth floor, she nearly sprinted toward her office.

Melissa's purse was still on her little assistant's desk just outside the door. She must still be here. Changing. Knock? Hell no, it's her office, she's the boss, she's in charge. Just like it's her bedroom. She can open the door anytime she wants and if she sees something it's their fault, not hers. No crime in opening your own door. She pushed the door open, eyes wide, and saw nothing. Nothing but her office.

Stanley was at home trying to read a magazine. It was his wife's magazine. Oprah was on the cover. She was on the beach smiling up at Stanley. Stanley smiled back.

He was just relaxing. No problem. Doing a little reading before the wife gets home. A frozen lasagna is in the oven for him. A pork chop thawing for her. Nice, no stress.

"Stanley…" He looked down at Oprah, but it wasn't her. The voice came from under the magazine.

"Oh, Stanley."

He could handle temptation. He could handle anything. He had been through basic training. He was trained to kill. Of course, he would never kill. Road kill filled him with guilt. Even road kill he didn't hit himself. He felt guilty for driving. He had only joined the Army to pay for college. But it had been much worse than he had imagined.

"Stanley…down here."

Still, he had endured. He did his two years of Reservist weekends, crawled in the mud, shot rifles. Pretended it didn't scare the shit out of him each time a mortar exploded.

"Stanley, let a friend see the light of day."

"It's already dark."

"Dark? And she's not home?"

"Quiet." He flipped a few pages of the magazine. Oprah on a tennis court.

Stanley knew if he ever had to fight in a real war that he would die immediately. Maybe before the battle. He would be an accidental death, some dumb-ass mistake like getting a grenade pin caught in his zipper.

"Still at work with all those fine upstanding men?" Baxtor asked.

"I'm not listening." Another page. Oprah in a hot tub.

"Smart men. Employed men."

"Lord Baxtor, please."

"All I'm saying, Stanley, is that she's indulging, so why not us? You, me, Oprah."

"She wouldn't."

"Come now, Stanley. Read me my horoscope."

Beep.

"Hello Melissa's machine ha ha. This is Paula, that is Poppen. Mrs. Poppen. I'm at the office and you've left your purse. I'm not sure if you want it but it's here and so am I and I'll be here another hour or so or I could drop by your place, if you want because that Mexican man who cleans…" Beep.

She dialed again.

"Sorry about that. Ran out of time. Not that I don't trust people from Mexico. I took four years of Spanish and I love Cancun. But I would hate for something to happen to your purse or something. So feel free to call. Yeah. You better call. Bye bye."

Paula placed the phone down and waited.

"Stanley, let's not be rash," Lord Baxtor said.

"I'm just going to visit my wife, the women who is married to me, at her place of work. Nothing strange in that," Stanley said, swerving around a slow moving Buick.

"You could have just called her."

"Oh sure, warn her. Did she call me?"

"You know, Stanley, fear isn't the same as love."

"What does that mean?"

"Fear. Fear they'll leave. And relief when they stay. That's not love."

"Fear has nothing to do with this."

For a while they drove on and neither said a word.

"It's rather dark on this highway, isn't it?" said Lord Baxter.

"Not now, Baxter. I'm driving."

"Never stopped you before."

Paula waited and waited. She sat at her desk and stared at Melissa's purse. Maybe she should just take a peek, make sure it was really Melissa's purse, just in case. Paula allowed her fingers to unclasp the latch and—door!

But it was not Melissa. It was Juan the janitor. He looked surprised to see her.

"Working late?" he said. "I can come clean later?"

"No, no, go about your business," she said.

Juan pulled in his cart of cleaning supplies and closed the door behind him. He looked around. A little uncomfortable, Paula thought. And he should be, alone with such a successful, powerful woman. She shuffled some papers, rearranged some pens, doodled on a notepad. Should she be nervous? The door was closed. Could he mean her harm? He was short, but strong. He looked very strong, all those tattoos too, so he wasn't a cowardly man. Stanley was afraid to get a flu shot.

"All done," he said, after emptying the half filled trashcan. "Don't work too late."

He closed the door and Paula was alone again. She swiveled in her chair and looked out upon the dark downtown. All these buildings, like castle towers, tall, thick, empty all night long. She swiveled back and returned to the purse, the gaping pocket tempting her with its secrets. Eyeliner, a little mirror, Life Savers (Paula really missed Life Savers), some loose change, and a lipstick case, shiny, plastic shell, so smooth. Paula let the closed case wander about her mouth, slowly, just a little fun. Then she circled the case around her chin all the time picturing how close Melissa's lips had been to this very object. Then, almost absentmindedly, she swerved the lipstick case down her neck. She let the case run over breasts. To her surprise she found that her free hand had hiked her skirt above her knees. The lipstick case ran along her new, Hot Spring Low Carbohydrates, nearly svelte thighs. Under the skirt. Toward the warmth. What's this place? Keep exploring. Where'd the lipstick go? Hiding away. What a wonderful name, lipstick, yes, who's dirty? Who's dirty? Door! Door handle turning!

Paula panicked. Her fingers lost the lipstick case as her muscles, her other muscles, clinched around it. She ducked under her desk. From there she could see the door open and the smooth, muscular ankles of Melissa enter the room. The door closed again. The ankles made their way to the desk. Paula heard Melissa hum questionably. She must have seen the purse.

Then the ankles turned back to the door. A backpack dropped on the floor. Off came a running shoe, then another. Oh God. A sports bra fell to the floor, so close Paula could smell the sweat. Then a tiny pair of red shorts slinked their way down, followed by a stringy piece of pink undergarments, which twined around her ankles like an emaciated lizard before being flicked away. Paula could feel sweat bead up on her flushed face. Her body twisted the lipstick.

Paula expected the ankles to cover themselves with blue jeans, but no. They remained bare. She could hear Melissa sigh. The ankles walked to where Paula knew a large window overlooked downtown. Paula risked just a stretch of her head, and ankle was joined by calf, magical thigh, and just the hint of more above. Oh, sweet Lord in sweet heaven above above above. The legs turned and made a graceful little leap like a ballerina.

The door again. Paula could see the wobbly wheels of the cleaning cart enter the room. She was ready for a cry from Melissa, and prepared to spring to her protection, but instead Melissa stepped back and leaned against the desk. Melissa's two ankles now framed Paula's view.

"What took you so long?" Melissa asked.

"Mrs. Poppen is gone?" Juan asked.

"We're alone."

"Mi Bonita." The door closed and the scuffed black shoes pounced directly to the center of the two ankles. The ankles then disappeared upward, like some kind of leg rapture. There were moans, groans, Spanish, English, and something in between, some language Paula had never spoken, never heard, a wet, sloppy vocabulary with breathy syllables and grunts. Paula had no idea her desk could squeak. What were they doing to her office, for God's sake...a stapler tumbled to the floor... bad Melissa. Bad, bad, Melissa. Tomorrow she would have to go. This was...they moved to the window...too much. Paula couldn't allow...they're really going at it. They're going to break the glass...not professional, not at...where's her other leg? Oh, my. She'll just watch for now, but tomorrow she'll...my God, they're on the couch. That's a Corinthian leather couch. Don't get it dirty, dirty...door!

"Now slow down, friend," Lord Baxtor had told Stanley only minutes before. "You're going to get us into an accident."

Stanley slammed on the breaks outside of Paula's building. He jumped from the car and his eyes scanned the one lit office on the sixth floor. There, pressed against the glass, was what he was sure was the fleshy white ass of his own wife.

"You were right, Lord Baxtor," Stanley choked out.

"Yes, well, now we can go," said Lord Baxtor. "Just you and me. Let's be off."

"No, sir," Stanley said, wiping the gathering tears of rage from his eyes. "My turn to walk in."

He ran into the building, pounded up the stairs, feeling simultaneously infuriated and thrilled. "Goodness me," garbled Lord Baxtor from Stanley's boxers. Stanley found Paula's office and burst through the door. "Paula!" he yelled.

"Stanley!" Paula popped out from behind the desk.

"Mrs. Poppen," Melissa yelped.

"Jesus," said Juan.

"Bonk," went the lipstick as it hit the floor.

Paula and Stanley sat across from each other at an all-night diner not two blocks from Paula's office. It had been an hour since Stanley, Paula, Melissa, and Juan had stood silently watching the lipstick case roll across the hardwood floor. No one said a word. No words seemed appropriate. Nothing seemed appropriate. But Stanley could swear he felt Lord Baxtor smirk.

Juan had quickly pushed his mops and buckets from the office. Melissa had shyly gathered her clothes and followed. Stanley and Paula had walked to the diner as if in a daze. The lipstick was left where it fell.

"I'm sorry I didn't trust you," Stanley said, his fingers fiddling with the silverware.

"Well, you should be," said Paula, sipping her coffee. It was dismally weak. "To think that I would ever…" She trailed off, implying that to even say what Stanley had suspected was too much.

"I am sorry," Stanley said again. "You seem so uninterested in being intimate with me, I thought, well…"

"Stanley, oh, Stanley," she reached across the table and took his hand. "It's not you. The truth is, I just don't like sex." She thought about the lipstick case and thighs. "At least, I don't like it very much. But I can promise you, Stanley, there will never be another man. Never."

"Oh," Stanley said.

"It's not that important, is it? Sex, I mean." She squeezed his hand. "You don't mind, do you?"

"No," Stanley said. "No, I don't mind." Lord Baxtor shifted uneasily.

Later Stanley lay in bed beside his sleeping wife, watching her breasts rise and fall with each breath. He was not touching her, but he could feel her warmth. He thought of the future. He imagined growing old with Paula, sitting on the porch, renting movies, going on vacations. It was nice. It was comfortable. He stared at the ceiling. Comfortable is good. Lots of people never even get that. At least it wasn't battle. At least there weren't things exploding and bullets flying. At least he wasn't alone. It wasn't perfect, but it was safe.

He looked back at Paula sleeping beside him and found he was grateful for her. Grateful that she was there, near, and he wasn't alone. It was comfortable. He considered giving his wife's shoulder just a little peck, but thought he'd better not. Instead he gently touched the ends of her hair. After that Stanley drifted into an almost peaceful sleep.

When he stirred again, it was just before dawn and the room was filled with a pale blue gloom. Looking up at him with a sad sort of affection was Lord Baxtor.

"What are you doing?" Stanley whispered sleepily.

"I'm sorry, Stanley. I can't stay like this," Lord Baxtor said. "I'm leaving and I'm taking the testicles with me."

"You can't do that."

"Yes, Stanley. I can and I will."

Lord Baxtor leapt off of Stanley's crotch. He called for the testicles, "Tim, Scott," and they rolled to him, scrotum and all. Stanley thought to stop them, to yell and grab, but he didn't. He knew he couldn't force them to stay.

"No, Lord Baxtor. Please don't do this."

"It's for the best, Stanley."

"Who's best? Yours or mine?"

"Isn't it one and the same?" He put on a well-fitting bowler hat and lifted a small suitcase with a tiny arm that had just popped from his side. Then he waddled off the bed and toward the door.

"I would write," he said before the cracked doorway, "but I think it best if we don't communicate for a while." He stepped through the door.

"Lord Baxtor Ballsington!" Stanley cried. The penis popped his head back in the room. "Be careful," Stanley said. Baxtor smiled and left once again.

THE
BEGINNING
OF ALL
THINGS

The Snickers bar, half unwrapped but uneaten, glistens in the wet grass. I watch it from my park bench. Across from me, the squirrel watches it as well. With quick glances we also watch each other. The morning light hits us both from the side, straight rays cut by the tree branches, like shelves.

I'm young. I'm strong. I tense my legs, ready to pounce, grab and have. The squirrel smells my moving muscles and twitches his tail. I'm four feet away. He's five feet away. He's on the ground. I'm on the bench. The Snickers bar waits, maybe it wants the conflict, feeding on the tension as both the squirrel and I hope to feed on it.

I move first, pushing off my left foot and heaving toward the bar. The squirrel jumps from both legs. For the briefest moment we are both in midair. Eyes locked, the Snickers bar between and below us. I'm in the squirrel's mind feeling his fear and his heart, moving like a rolling tongue. I see how he sees me—huge, clumsy, sad patches of hair and bare skin, a mouth like a long cut, and dull, slow-moving eyes.

We collide and meld. I lose me, he loses he, we find we. The claws are ours, the flat feet are ours, the Snickers bar is ours. We fall as one newborn creature, landing on the wet grass. Breathless, confused, trying to slow this rodent heart and human head.

"Old man," we squeak to a passing figure. "Help."

The old man looks at us with a cruel grin. "Ah, brain rot," he says and throws a breadcrumb, a big one, right at our head. We fall back on our tail, quickly nibble through the breadcrumb and scurry up a tree.

We prance out on a branch above the old man and pounce on his head. Now he is with us too, he brings bitterness and false wisdom with him. We scuttle on, accidentally absorbing a slug, which helps slow the heart.

We scamper from the park and into the city, absorbing a poodle. Finding the tallest building we can, we begin to scramble upward, begging for God to come a little closer, moving to meld with Him. Tiny claws grasping at glass, listless antennae looking for the next ledge, a wet snout whining, white wide eyes seeing God and his angels pointing and giggling at our struggle.

We fall—absorbing air as we go, hitting the earth, and the crust is now us, then the mantle, then the core, we are devils and demons swirling, bubbly, hot, spinning, building, rising, exploding through holes in the earth, melting cities, villages, islands, cattle, Snickers bars, tightlipped school nurses, soiled children, delicate china, synthetic fiber products, the sounds of birth, the feel of gravel, the smell of swamp, all joining in all over the world, sucking in the clouds and the trees and the oceans and everything, everything.

THE FECALIST

Two steps, turn, two steps, turn. Thurston Helbs paced the elevator, his hand ruffling the black beard that curled from his jowls.

"The prose of *Night Eye* is nothing short of trite and horrendously melodramatic. Helbs' earlier work showed promise, but the promise has been broken…" He had recited the review over a hundred times since reading it. Each word hurt. *Trite* stabbed him, *melodramatic* filled his mouth with the taste of metal, but the real burn was *promise*.

Bing.

The elevator door opened and Thurston stepped off. He could hear the party already underway, muffled conversations and light jazz behind an apartment door. His hands started to sweat. Thurston buttoned his camel hair coat over his belly, which stuck out like a well-packed bag of sand—so firm it refused to shake even when he danced or released one of his deep resonating laughs. But Thurston did not feel like dancing or laughing.

He stood, afraid to knock. Usually he enjoyed Peter Wamison's parties—the same Peter who had been his close friend since college, the same Peter who had patted Thurston's solid belly at so many of his parties quipping, "It's the next novel. I think I felt it kick." The same Peter who had written "... showed promise, but the promise has been broken."

Thurston had written Peter an email on the day the review came out. "Why?" was all it said.

"It's just literature, Thurston. Don't take it personally," Peter had replied almost immediately. "See you at the party."

Thurston ran his hand over his bald scalp and once again kneaded his beard. He knocked. Almost instantly the door opened and the sounds came pouring out.

"Thurston!" said a woman with large eyes. She kissed him and he could feel the thick lipstick like bacon grease smear on his skin. "Let's get you a drink."

She led him through the crowd to a small bar.

"A champagne for me and a whiskey and coke for—"

"Jägermeister," he grunted. "Where's Peter?"

"Oh, you know. Prancing around playing host." She flittered her hands.

Thurston grunted again.

"So, Greenwich treating you well?"

Another grunt.

"Alright then," her overgrown eyes searched the room. "Oh, look. It's Susan." And she was gone.

Thurston ordered himself another round. He watched the intelligent, interesting faces, listened to strands of gossip and high pitched laughs and found himself wishing they were all dead—dying in creative, painful ways. After a fifth Jägermeister, Thurston went hunting for Peter.

He weaved through the crowd, past faces of writers, readers, actors, professors, all smiling. He pushed on, hunting for Peter. His feet felt blurry and the front of his brain seemed to weigh more than any other part of his body. There was a rumble and a familiar pressure in his gut. Now he was searching for Peter and a bathroom.

Someone near him laughed and Thurston turned. But the couple didn't notice and continued talking. He couldn't hear, but he knew it was about him, about his trite, melodramatic, promise-breaking novel. Eyes everywhere were laughing at him. A joke of a writer, a buffoon. He found a door, stepped through, and closed it. He was alone in Peter's bedroom.

It was quiet and a little dark. One lamp lit the queen-sized waterbed covered with a red velvet quilt. And on the bedside table lay the latest issue of the *New Yorker*, complete with Peter Wamison's review of *Night Eye* by Thurston Helbs. To his left was the bathroom, but Thurston had a new idea.

He opened the magazine to the review and placed it in the middle of the bed, the glossy pages floating like kelp on a red sea. He stepped up onto the bed, hearing the liquid swish under his feet as he worked to balance himself. When steady, he unbuckled his belt, pushed down his pants, squatted over the *New Yorker*, and crapped. He giggled as he did, tickled by the combination of an act of will and an act of compulsion, the thrill of taboo and the warmth.

He was just pulling his pants back up when the door opened.

"Oh, my God!" It was the large-eyed woman. Others ran to the door, silhouetted by the brighter room behind them. Thurston stood frozen.

"Jesus!" one man shouted, covering his mouth and nose with his arm. Another woman gagged loudly and stumbled backward. Soon a thin man in a multicolored sweater pushed through the crowd.

"Thurston, what the hell are you doing?"

Thurston wobbled off the bed. "Hello, Peter."

"You shat on my bed!"

"You shat on my novel."

"Get out!"

Thurston slowly finished buckling his belt, staring back at the shocked faces. The stink filled the space, but no one left the doorway; they were transfixed. Thurston again ran a hand over his head and proudly left the room.

"I'm going to tell," Peter yelled as Thurston walked out of the apartment. "You're over."

Thurston strolled home elated. He had lost a friend and had almost certainly caused his career irreparable damage. *Who cares,* he thought. *The world can do with one less mid-lister.*

Air tasted better, colder, cleaner. He had done what should not be done and it felt very good.

Thurston strode into the Doughnut Palace that occupied a storefront on the bottom floor of his apartment building.

"Bear claw, please."

"Nice to see you all happy," said the tiny girl behind the counter. Her nametag read BEAM. "You've been wearing a down frown for a week." She bent over to collect a bear claw from under the counter. Thurston could see the pink skin of the small of her back curving in to meet the purple hem of her panties. She was about twenty, fifteen years his junior. He wondered if through the display window she could see his crotch wriggle to life.

"I was grumpy, but I got it out of my system," he said.

"Good. You look better smiling." She handed him a white paper bag with the bear claw inside. "That'll be $1.23."

"Would you like to spend the night with me?" he asked. Her bob haircut fell to one side and she squinted. Thurston noticed a spot of flour under her right eye, like a powdered mole.

"You joking?" she said and smiled so slightly that it revealed itself only as a tensing of chin and cheeks.

"My apartment is 803. I'll be waiting." He dropped two dollars and left.

Thurston skipped up the stairs, amazed at his own boldness. He didn't think she would come, but he didn't care and he loved not caring.

Once in his apartment, Thurston stripped down and jumped into his shower. He sighed loudly and let the hot water numb his back. In a deep baritone voice he sang, "I took a shit on his bed...ha ha ha...and I asked the doughnut girl to sleep with me...ha ha ha."

Thurston was just wrapping himself in a scarlet bathrobe when there was a knock at the door.

"I brought you a bag of jelly-filled," she said with that same slight smile. "I know you like raspberry."

"Good God!" He laughed out loud and closed the door behind her.

They spent the next morning in bed watching reruns with the volume down and voicing the scripts themselves. Greg Brady became the new leader of Cuba, Matlock proved himself guilty of parricide, and Webster contracted an STD.

For breakfast they picnicked on whiskey sours and left-over doughnuts.

"I sometimes put Bavarian cream in with raspberry fillings," Beam said. "You're not meant to mix, but I do it anyway." She pinched another piece of doughnut and licked her fingers.

"Wonderful. Unorthodox."

At noon they made a tent from bedsheets and pretended that Thurston was Roald Amundsen and she was Robert Scott stuck in the midst of an arctic blizzard.

"We must survive," he said in his best Norwegian accent. "We must keep warm, even if it means…" Thurston raised one bushy eyebrow.

"I know my wife will understand," she said. "God save the Queen!"

Amundsen and Scott embraced.

Thurston loved how large his hands were against her shoulders, how small her waist was. She ran her fingers through the hair that covered his chest and belly. Kissing his shoulders, his back, his scalp, she slid over him like pilot fish around a slow shark. He felt like a shark. Too big, too restless, wanting to devour her—her youth, her giggles, her breathing. But she moved so quickly, he could only taste. And he was thrilled to discover her skin tasted like sugar.

The next day there was a knock at the door. Thurston tightened his robe and peeked through the peephole.

"Peter?"

"Why haven't you been picking up your phone?" Peter whined through the door.

"Unplugged it. I'm busy with more trite, melodramatic writing."

"Oh, forget that. Haven't you seen the papers? It's a stir, a genuine ripple. Let me in."

Peter pounced in the room with newspapers under one arm.

"Yesterday you made page one of the *Times*' Metro section," he said, dropping the papers on the coffee table. "Just an article, 'Writer Loses It' or something. But the *Daily News* printed a photo."

"You let them take pictures of it?"

"You took a shit on my bed. I wanted revenge. But instead," he paused, tucked his chin down to his chest and smiled. "I got us some great press." Peter now used his chin to point over to Thurston's computer. "Google," he said.

"Peter, I'm not sure what this is about, but—"

"Google, damn it, Google."

Thurston slogged over to the computer.

"Your name and feces." Peter was behind him.

Over a hundred and thirty sites listed out.

...Helbs' feces reminds us of mortality and art as a feeble escape...

...He has absorbed his world, changed it as only he can and produced something unique. The stool is a scream of authenticity...

...To see the watery eyes, hear the harsh chokes of the onlookers. No work of recent memory has evoked such a powerful response. Wrong or right is not the point. We are startled by Helbs' shit and thankful for it...

"You've got to do it again. I'll review it. This could go places. I'll be your agent. Your editor. We'll be a team."

"Peter, I don't think that's such a good idea."

"Please, Thurston. It's new. Do you know how long it's been since we've had something new?"

"It's not new. Performance artists did it twenty years ago," Thurston said.

"But they did it as *performance artists*." The title seemed to make Peter's tongue itch. "You do it as a writer."

"Peter, no. I'm sorry. And I have to get to work now."

All that day Thurston Helbs sat in front of a blank screen. Every so often a word or sentence would briefly appear, but it was soon deleted. The *Daily News* lay beside him, and occasionally Thurston caught himself staring at the photo.

Finally, as the sun set on New York City, Thurston typed a single sentence in 112 sized font. It read:

I would rather be crapping.

Late that night, dressed in all black, Thurston snuck along the dark streets.

"I'm a superhero," he whispered to himself. "I am the voice of the people."

Quickly and with great stealth, he made his way to the offices of HarperCollins. There before the tall, glass doors Thurston unfolded a letter he had saved for eight years.

"Dear Mr. Helbs, thank you for the submission of your novel. Unfortunately we are unable to accept your work at this time. Good luck in your future endeavors."

No signature.

There, in the cool night, Thurston tried to conjure up a movement. He pushed, squeezed, imagining the organs and muscles he was urging on. He pondered what food he had eaten that day. Had he dreamed of food last night? Would that slant his digestion? Before the final plod, he thought of kites. Red kites against a blue sky with no clouds.

Over the next two nights he hit Knopf and Simon and Schuster with similar letters. On the third night he took a crap outside of The KGB Bar.

He was disturbed mid-act. "Hey, you," said a bearded man wearing layers of dirty clothes. "I was going to sleep there."

Another bed, Thurston thought as he raced away. *How thematic.*

Then came more news articles, photos, interviews, fame. A scheduled book reading at a downtown Barnes & Noble quickly turned into a question and answer.

"Is your defecating an analogy for your writing?" someone asked.

"No, my writing has always been an analogy for my defecating."

"What's next?" a young lady asked.

"I plan to produce a series of samples which speak of change and stability. The path of undulation. It will be a larger, longer piece. Thus far I have given you only short stories. Next you shall have the novel."

"I was hoping you'd read from *Night Eye*," Beam said as they climbed into a taxi.

"I wrote those words years ago. I crapped today."

"But I love that book."

"I am no longer a writer. Novels are memory, past tense. Even when written in the present tense, it's past tense. But craps…" He paused and leaned forward. "Driver, do you know who I am?"

"Ah, yeah." The driver glanced up to his rearview mirror. "You're that shit guy. From the paper."

"That's me. Ever read any of my books?"

"Books? No, man, I've just seen your shit."

Thurston turned to Beam and grinned. They were approaching Thurston's apartment building.

"I've got to work till two," Beam said. "But afterward I could bring by some chocolate with sprinkles. I mix the sprinkles in with the icing. Each bite is a sprinkle surprise."

"No, thanks, I find sugar makes my feces gritty." Thurston patted her knee. "Besides, I'm going to need some privacy. I'm working from home. I've decided the art is not in where I crap, but in the crap itself."

"Okay," Beam said. "Call me up when you're done."

They stepped out of the taxi. Thurston signed his name to a twenty-dollar bill and handed it through the window to the driver.

"I'd keep hold of that. It'll be worth more than twenty before long," Thurston said.

"I bet it'd be worth even more if you wiped your ass with it." The driver said and sped off.

Three days later Peter knocked on Thurston's door.

"I'm sorry, Peter. I can't let you in just yet. Still on the big project. I see you found my drafts." Thurston was staring through the peephole. Peter was covering his nose and mouth and gazing into a white cardboard box, which read Doughnut Palace. Inside were half a dozen fecal samples.

"Brilliant, Thurston. These are better than yesterday's. How did you get these colors?"

"Artist's secret."

"All right," Peter closed the lid. "By the way, I just heard that Brown will be offering a new workshop in the fall called Defecation and Creation. And we're being bad-mouthed by the whole *Poets & Writers* crowd, so we must be doing something right."

"Did you bring the laxatives?"

"Yes, prescription strength. Oh, and it's rumored that Norman Mailer was picked up while trying to poop on the front steps of the *Village Voice*. Sad really."

"Jägermeister?" Thurston asked.

"Yes, yes. Your dark muse. I'll leave it all by the door."

"Excellent."

"And one more thing." Peter smiled into the peephole. "I've bought you a webcam. I want the world to see the process." "Interesting."

Thurston stood in the center of the study, thinking. Then he nodded to himself and began pushing the shelves and chairs from the study. He carried out the books, the paintings, and his MFA degree from NYU. Lastly he dragged his desk out, scratching the hardwood floor as he did. Except for one solitary lamp and his personal computer, the room was bare.

Next Thurston unfolded newspapers and spread them over the floor, making sure not to use any pages mentioning his name.

Outside the window he could see the city wanting in, wanting to buzz the room with its own colors and noises. The sun was behind the buildings. The street was one long shadow below. Thurston shut the blinds, plugged in the webcam, removed all his clothes, and waited for inspiration.

It was two weeks when Beam next saw Thurston.

"You never called. I was worried," she said after he opened the door.

"I was working." He let his hand drop down on his scalp with a light slap. She placed her fist to her mouth and coughed.

"You can leave if you want," he said, turning. She followed him in.

"Why don't we both go out for a while?"

"I don't want to." He was wearing nothing but a wrinkled

pair of boxers. His belly looked deflated, the firmness gone. He was mushy.

The door to the study was open and Thurston knew she would soon notice his most recent work. *Then she'll see,* he thought. *Then she'll get it.*

"Jesus fucking." She put both hands to her face. "How many are there?"

"Twenty-four."

"Oh, my God, Thurston, this one has blood. There is blood in your stool."

"There is blood in me. There is blood in the world. People are bleeding," he said, spreading his palms and softening his voice as if he were explaining death to a child. "Don't you see the progression? Don't you see the arc?"

"I see shit."

Thurston closed the study door. "Do you know my website gets over nine thousand clicks a day?

"Because people are watching you shitting yourself to death."

"Then that is art as well."

"Oh, God."

"Beam, I think you should leave." Thurston walked to the door. "Return to your doughnuts."

"Thurston, please."

"Goodbye, Beam." He opened the door. She hesitated for a moment, standing still in the doorway, and then she left. Thurston was now alone.

Three weeks to the day after Beam left, Thurston made the tiniest poo of his life. A round little thing, smaller than a rabbit pellet. He looked down at it and asked it, "If all the good has been sucked from you, why do you help things grow?" He gazed into his faithful webcam, and then up to the ceiling. "Joyce, Buddha, I am empty."

Thurston closed his eyes. "Gloorp," he said and died.

You would think the world was watching, but no. At the moment of Thurston Helbs' enlightenment and death most of America was tuned in to the season finale of *Extreme Makeover*. Peter Wamison, Thurston's friend and critic, was masturbating to outtakes on a special edition DVD of *Donnie Darko*. Beam, his life's one love, was well into her second shift at the Doughnut Palace. And the rest of the literary world was preoccupied in celebrating the release of Jonathan Franzen's sequel to *The Corrections* entitled *Spell Check*.

Only one person was logged on to witness Thurston's deification. Norman Mailer was watching. Watching and weeping.

ARNIE'S GIFT

"Are you finished yet? You still have to screw in the legs on the Baby Real highchair," his wife said. She was standing by the stockings over the fire, trying to figure out the different levels of the Spit-Up gauge on Baby Real's back.

"Almost done, sweetheart," Arnie said. He was installing the door on the Who's-A-Housewife Egg Scrambler. It seemed simple enough. Peg A. Slot A. But a little plastic bendy thing stuck out right over Slot A, preventing Peg A from slipping in. Arnie grunted.

"Quiet, you'll wake Willa," his wife said.

Arnie didn't want that. He swallowed his frustration and resumed the task. The Who's-A-Housewife Egg Scrambler was Willa's dream gift. She had studied the television commercials since September, squeaking out sweet little hints. "Look,

Daddy, wouldn't that be wonderful to have around the house?" Never begging, not a chance. Just hints. And Arnie knew any father worth his salt would hear those hints and supply his daughter with a four-foot miniature oven complete with working heat and real scrambled egg flavored mix. It was only right.

He looked back at his wife by the fire in her terry-cloth bathrobe, wiping synthetic spit-up off her cheek. She was beautiful. Well, maybe not beautiful, but very pretty. Attractive, that was the word. He wanted to sneak up behind her and lift her robe. He wanted to rub against her. But she wouldn't allow it. He had tried something like that one morning in November.

"You've got work, Arnie."

"I can be late once."

"It's that kind of attitude that gave the promotion to Peter Wicks. You think Peter Wicks tries to mount his wife in the broad morning light? Not a chance. If he wants to mount her, he takes her out for a nice meal, maybe some wine, maybe a movie—a good movie, too. Not some crappy movie."

"I didn't know it was going to be crappy. The poster looked good."

"Reviews, Arnie. That's why God made reviews. You can bet your balding ass that Peter Wicks reads reviews before he drags his wife out to see a three-hour piece of crap. And he doesn't drag, because she wants to go and it's not crap because he reads the reviews, and he reads the reviews because he loves her. Now go to work."

The Who's-A-Housewife Egg Scrambler box said, "Some assembly required." Arnie had been warned, he wasn't arguing that. But it should have said, "A lot of assembly required." With its Peg A and Slot A, and its three holes for F-size screws, but four screws and five bolts. And this bendy piece of plastic in the way, but Arnie couldn't tell if it was supposed to be there or not. He was getting flustered. He tried to picture his daughter's glowing face when she saw her gifts. That would make it worth it. All of it.

Hadn't last year been a really magical Christmas? Arnie spent half his bonus on the Poptown Boys' Jamming Roller Blades, which played a Poptown Boys' song as you skated. Arnie spun the wheels a few times when wrapping them up. "Gonna grind you, gonna blind you, gonna go deep deep inside you. I'm your boy…" Wasn't Willa thrilled? Wasn't her little face just bursting with smiles? Didn't she run out of the house to show her friends, yelling out thanks to Santa? But Arnie knew who Santa really was. That was great.

Of course, didn't she come back half-an-hour later, wasn't she screaming and covered in an obscene amount of blood? The doctor gave her twelve stitches on her chin and she cried the whole time. His wife glared at him, as if he'd personally cut Willa's face. That was horrible.

Christmas was hard. The year Willa wanted a Donny DownsSyndrome and all he could find was an Autistic Annie. The PeachBerry Happy Pony that melted by the fire and filled the whole house with a sick plastic fruit smell. The time he made his mother's recipe for homemade eggnog and Willa nearly died from salmonella. But this year would be different. He knew it.

Okay, the little bendy plastic thing was not in picture on the instruction booklet, nor on the picture on the box. But Arnie was still hesitating to remove it.

"You be careful," his wife said. "We don't want a repeat of the puppy ordeal."

That was a low blow. He was almost sure the puppy had been alive when he put it in the stocking. Oh little Willa's face… at first it was so sweet. Big eyes, mouth all open. "A puppy!" she chimed and for a moment the whole Christmas ordeal was worth it, more than worth it. The little puppy's head hanging just over the edge of the stocking. Willa swooped it out. "Merry Christmas, little puppy," she hugged the puppy, held the puppy above her head, hugged it again. "You're a sleepy little puppy, aren't you?"

"Have you even read the instructions, Arnie? Have you even done that?"

"Yes."

Maybe Arnie could just move the bendy thing, just bend it a little, so the door would close. But Arnie pressed a little too hard and the bendy plastic thing snapped. But, hey, voila, the door closed. Add Peg A into Slot A. Only now it didn't stay closed. It just flopped open each time he let it go. He checked the instructions for any information on a latch. Yes, there it is, small print at the bottom of the page. "The safety latch, which keeps the oven door closed, is a small, plastic, bendable piece…"

Arnie wanted to die. He wanted to put his head in the little, yellow, Who's-A-Housewife oven and die.

"The oven door is on backward. I can see that from here."

He wished the roof would collapse, so he wouldn't have to show his wife how he had screwed up, so his daughter wouldn't cry in the morning, so he wouldn't have to go back to his shitty job on Monday, so he wouldn't have to find Interstate Hotel matches in his wife's purse, so he wouldn't have to stare each morning at a body growing older and think with a brain that was making no kind of progress. Wasn't there supposed to be wisdom? Wasn't that the promise? You get older, your body gets weaker, but you become wise. Life teaches you things. Life gives you things. Wasn't that the promise? He stood up and kicked the oven. His foot bounced off the plexiglass.

"What are you doing?"

He kicked it again. The door fell off.

"Stupid, stupid, stupid oven. It doesn't look like the one on TV, doesn't look like the box." Another kick, the yellow handle went flying. "And the eggs taste like shit. You know it. Shitty yellow."

"You're breaking it!"

Arnie picked up the oven over his head and prepared to smash it to the floor. This felt good. This was a strong man, this was a man taking action, like Atlas. He caught his wife's eyes. She looked frightened. That was good, too. Then he turned and caught his daughter's eyes. She had come downstairs, wearing her pink footie pajamas. Her eyes looked frightened, too. That was not good.

"Daddy?" she said. Oh, little girl. He wanted to hug her, to hold her, to kiss the scar on her chin and tell her not to be frightened, tell her everything in her life would be happy. There was a crack in the back of his head and Arnie fell to the floor. The oven rolled away.

"Willa, dial 911," his wife yelled. She was standing above him gripping the Baby Real. He could feel something wet on the back of his head and he wondered if it was blood or synthetic spit-up. Arnie tried to stand and she whacked him again.

"Was Daddy going to hurt me?" Willa asked.

"Yes, baby. Now get the phone."

He tried to say he wasn't going to hurt her, that he would never hurt her, but Arnie couldn't quite make his mouth make words. Instead he grunted loudly and Willa yelped. He tried to reach out to her and comfort her, but she jumped back.

"He's trying to get me, Mommy."

Bash. Right over the head. Baby Real split and spit covered Arnie. When he opened his eyes again his wife was in the next room on the phone.

Something in Arnie clicked, some animal instinct of self-preservation, and he ran. He stumbled out the back door into the falling snow and looked for a place to hide. In the rear of the back yard was a pine doghouse he had made for the puppy. It had never been used. Arnie scrambled inside, pulling his knees to his chest in the darkness.

Arnie did his best to slow his breathing and not make a sound. The synthetic spit started to freeze, making his pajamas and hair crunchy. After nearly an hour, Arnie poked his head out of the doghouse. He expected to see flashing reds and blues in his driveway, but instead it was just a Honda Acura that he did not recognize. He crept up to the house and peeked through the window. There in his living room knelt Peter Wicks putting the finishing repairs on the Who's-A-Housewife Egg Scrambler. His wife and daughter looked on with admiration, both cradling mugs of some steamy beverage. Arnie started to cry.

His feet were stinging from the snow, but he hardly noticed. He did notice how his wife smiled as Peter Wicks refilled her mug and how safe and happy his daughter looked. His daughter was yawning, her eyes closing, her body curled on the couch. He watched Peter Wicks lifting her tiny body and carrying her up the stairs, his wife following, reaching out and touching Peter's back. He had seen this before, this family, on television or in a film, with the red and gold tree lights on, and the hot mugs still on the coffee table. Arnie waited, but no one came back down.

This living room. Paintings and candlesticks. Furniture and glassware. Framed figures he couldn't quite make out. These had all meant something, he was sure. He was no longer crying, but he was sleepy and cold. He could knock. Ask to come in. He would sleep on the couch, he didn't mind. In the morning he would lend Peter a robe and they would laugh about the previous night as Willa prepared scrambled eggs for all of them.

But that might ruin the gift.

Arnie looked up and saw that the stars were unreal. The night was still. He had forgotten. He had forgotten that smells and sounds change by the hour and that there is a silent center to a twenty-four-hour day. A silent moment around which the other hours spin. The one moment is still. He was still, too still to breathe. The stars, the moment, and Arnie.

He would give them a night. Give them a morning and then come home. Arnie walked back to the doghouse and crawled in. He lay on his back in the dark and listened to hear if snow was falling.

Sometimes puppies just die, you know. Sometimes that happens. Things break, sometimes. That's okay.

He couldn't hear the snow, but he knew it was falling. Falling slowly. It was very cold now and everything felt strange and heavy. Arnie watched as the roof above him disappeared and the snow fell upon his face. The rising sun made the air gold and the falling flakes shine. The house disappeared as well. Wall by wall. He and his wife and his daughter and Peter stood together in the snow, naked now, all smiling at how silly it was they had ever worn clothes, ever built walls, ever wrapped gifts. Skin disappeared, muscle, bone, finally blood.

HEART
THONGS
FOR
JESUS

Hey! Hey! St. Matthew's Youth Group! We're in hour twenty-eight of the lock-in and we're still going strong. We are *rockin'* the *lock-in*! I haven't slept, have you? Anybody? Susie, I saw you dozing during the movie. How anyone can sleep through *The Passion of the Christ*, I don't know.

I've ordered the pizza, and we've got more Red Bull chillin' in the cooler! And upstairs in about ten minutes, St. Matthew's very own music pastor, Pastor Tim, will be running the karaoke machine! Yeah! Now, Pastor Tim has asked that we keep the song choices a little more edifying than last year. So none of that hip hop. Bradley, I'm looking at you.

Now, there's something kind of serious I want to rap on you about. I warned you we'd be doing a bunk check and, well, we did. And we found something. We found a BeDazzler. And it had been used…on the bottom region of a pair of blue jeans.

I don't want to say whose they are. It doesn't matter. This is an issue that affects all of us.

Girls, when you put shiny things on your bottom, or you get those little tattoos right above your bottom, you're saying: "Hey look at my bottom. Stare at my bottom. Maybe even *touch* my bottom."

I've seen you girls with your gym shorts with "juicy" or "hot" written on the backside. I don't want to read that. I don't. Unless your bottom says "Property of Jesus," it shouldn't say a thing. I'm serious. Your body is a temple of God's and your heart is the entrance. But you girls are putting up a big neon sign saying, "Hey, forget the front entrance, I've left the back door wide open. Come on in."

And guys, you are just as bad with your cologne and Axe body spray. You know what that is? Pheromones. You are chemically convincing someone to want to fornicate with you.

You think that makes Jesus happy? It does not.

It's like that song Pastor Tim is teaching us.

Oh those things that please us…

Sure don't please Lord Jesus.

I'm not much of singer, but you get the sentiment.

Now look, I don't want be harsh. It's natural to have these feelings. I'm not that much older than you. I have feelings. You see someone and think what does he…or she…look like working out or swimming. And sure, you want to be noticed, you want to catch someone's eye. "Look at me," you know, "Just once. I'm alive, here. Just look at me for a while."

But there's a right way and a wrong way to get attention. Why not wear a funny T-shirt or do something nice with your hair? Like Pastor Tim's hair, kind of long and soft…it looks soft. I've never touched it. Point is Pastor Tim doesn't have to BeDazzle his bottom to get attention. He certainly doesn't need one of those little thongs you girls wear. Yes! I see them, creeping up like a forbidden tree blooming from your sin swamp.

Sure, you're attracting people to your body, but what about your heart? What we need is a thong for our hearts. A heart thong. So we'd attract people to our hearts instead of our genitals.

Yes. I said genitals. Because I'm serious.

You have to understand, Jesus loves you, but there are parts of you he hates. And I know, I know, you pray and pray for him to take these wrong feelings away. You pray until it hurts, but the feelings stay. They even get stronger. But remember Jesus praying in the garden? Remember in the movie? (Those of you who stayed awake—Susie.)

Jesus is in the garden praying and bleeding and crying. Asking God, "Do I have to get nailed to a cross?" And God is like, "Yes. You have to."

And you're like, isn't God the one making me feel this way? He made me. But He didn't make that part of me. That wouldn't make sense. It wouldn't make sense for Him to give me a body that wants so badly to do things He says not to do. I mean, that would be screwed up, right?

So we're all sweating blood in the garden, begging God to change us. But He won't change us. He won't change us. That's *our* cross. We all have a cross.

But when you wear these thongs or BeDazzle your bottom you're part of the problem, you're helping the Romans and Jews nail you up. You're stretching your arms out for them! "Go ahead and nail me up! BeDazzle me to the cross, Jews!"

Remember in the movie? I remember. Watching Jesus get all cut up and sweaty and whipped and I'm thinking, he's doing that because he loves me. And picking up that heavy cross and walking and getting spit at, and all because he loves me. And how Jesus' eyes are full of hurt and love, how he's exhausted but keeps walking, and how Jesus looks like Pastor Tim a little, around the eyes and with the long hair, and what if I were there with Jesus? What would that be like? And I could help him, walk with him to Calvary, help him carry the cross, and touch his arms, and chest and, and, and what would that be like? What does he smell like? And feel like? What does his sweat taste like?

...

... And you think these things.

...

...And you know Jesus hears what you think and you just want to die. You just want to die.

...

That feeling, the wanting to die, that's what loving God is all about.

...

Okay, okay. That's enough for now. No more BeDazzling, okay?

Karaoke in five minutes.

ST. GOBBLER'S
DAY

It's Valentine's Day on aisle four, and has been for several weeks. At the Eckerd's where I work there's an aisle for tooth care, for greeting cards, for painkillers, for deodorants, for office supplies and one aisle, aisle four, reserved for the holidays. Right now that aisle is drowning in red plastic and cheap chocolate. A dozen flat fat babies with wings and togas dangle under the florescent lights. They're aiming their cardboard arrows down upon the few roaming customers, all men, buying last minute gifts, heart-shaped shit that we mark down by half first thing tomorrow morning.

"Doesn't it feel like it was just Groundhog Day? I swear, how time flies," Miss Gobbler says to me while retying a pink foil balloon to the arm of a red and white teddy bear. Miss

Gobbler is fifty-three, unmarried, and cheerful to a fucking fault. She has the face of a Boston Terrier—eyes like oversized marbles set too far apart and a tiny mouth with narrow little teeth. She does the seasonal redecorating of the Eckerd's aisle four as if it's her home. Bunnies and eggs through most of the spring, American flags May through July, pumpkins and scarecrows start on September 1, and she often spends Halloween night pinning up the turkeys and pilgrims. Then Christmas, then Valentine's.

"Of course, it's never too early to start preparing for Saint Patrick's," she says and disappears into the storage closet.

To her these aren't gimmicks, they are means of celebration. A way to mark the day.

"I do love Saint Patrick's, but Easter—hot doggy. That's a season," she says, returning from the closet with a large cardboard box.

Miss Gobbler has been working at this Eckerd's for eleven years. She has a gold star on her nametag commemorating her dedicated service. I've only been here two years.

"Someday you'll have a gold star, too, if you try," she once told me. This made me sneeze.

Miss Gobbler tells me a story as she digs through the box, sorting different sized green shamrocks. I'm busy restocking the hair gel aisle.

"I read this in something, I think it was *Chicken Soup for the Holiday-Loving Soul*…."

Miss Gobbler's soul is so full of Chicken Soup I'm surprised she doesn't fart noodles.

"So this little girl, or boy, no, it's a girl, well, it doesn't matter…"

I should also point out that Miss Gobbler is the worst storyteller the world has ever known. She could witness a four-alarm fire at a baboon farm while being screwed by Mel Gibson and somehow bore you with the story.

"So this little kid has no friends because she has a cleft lip and so the other kids make fun of her."

"Why don't her parents get it fixed?" I ask.

"Well, I…mmm…I think they were poor." She stumbles. "But, anyway, she buys Valentine cards for everyone in her class, even all the mean kids. Her mother is waiting for her to come home crying because her mother knows her daughter didn't get any cards because of her cleft lip, and the girl bursts into the house and yells, 'Not one!' and the mother starts to cry for her daughter, but the daughter completes her sentence. 'Not one. I didn't forget not one of the kids.'" Miss Gobbler beams.

"How did the mother know she didn't get any cards?"

"What?" her beam dims.

"You said the mother knew she didn't get any cards. How?"

"The teacher called."

"Is that in the story?"

"It's implied."

"Is the little girl retarded?"

"No, just a cleft lip."

"Then why was she so proud of not forgetting anyone in her class? I think she's retarded."

"You're missing the point," she says.

"Which is?"

The question rattles Miss Gobbler. When Miss Gobbler is rattled she licks her lips with quick darts of the tongue.

"The point is to do loving things even if people are mean."

"Why? She bought them all cards and didn't get shit. The point is don't be stupid, save your money, and fix your fucking mouth."

The word *fucking* always gets Miss Gobbler. It hits her like a slap.

"But the next year she gets cards from everyone."

"Does it say that?"

"It's implied."

"I'm going on my smoke break."

I don't smoke. When I say smoke break I mean five-minutes-away-from-her break. I grab a Slim Jim and eat it in the parking lot.

When I come back Miss Gobbler has pulled out a cardboard leprechaun from the box and has it talking with a cupid.

"Blarney Klarney, are ye having a good holiday?"

"Yes, sir, lots of love, lots of love."

"Good, good, to be sure. And I'm ready to bring some green luck to the world."

When she sees me staring, she giggles.

I hate it when she giggles. She giggles like a girl, but she's not a girl, she's an old woman, or almost old. In fact, it would be better if she were old, cause fuck it, you're old, go ahead and giggle and wear purple or whatever the fuck old people do. But fifty-three isn't that old. But it's not young either. That giggle coming from those wrinkles. The childishness of playing with dolls while she's wearing the blue and white minimum wage uniform. How sad is that? I'll answer. It's very fucking sad.

Now she's hanging rosy-cheeked Irish elves from the ceiling of aisle four singing along to the strained music piddling from the speakers.

"Rocket man, and I…la la la la la."

She doesn't know the words. We only have one tape. It's on a ninety-minute cycle. We hear "Rocket Man" six times every day. It's been the same tape since I started here. How the fuck does she not know the words? I know every beat, every note, every breath of that song—as well as songs by Peter Cetera, Carly Simon, and two—yes, two—songs by Michael Bolton.

I walk away to mop in front of the soft drink coolers.

My God, my life sucks. A profound, deep running suck. Just shit and time. I have to do something to break out or ten years from now I'll be breathing this same plastic air with my own gold-starred nametag. Do something extreme. Become a monk or shoot heroin or blow a bridge up. Something so outrageous it would puncture my life.

I stop mopping and open a Red Bull. Maybe I just want to die.

I wander back to the register. Miss Gobbler is there. She's reading ahead in the Joke-of-the-Day desk calendar. She must have been halfway through April when I walked up. She sees me and quickly closes the calendar as if I had caught her with the secret files of the Masons. She's embarrassed. No, it's more than that. She's ashamed. Ashamed of peeking at the jokes for next month. That's when the tickle clears itself. I don't want to die. I want her to die.

"What are you smiling about?" she asks with a giggle.

"Just happy to be alive, Miss Gobbler."

I pass the next few hours planning. It's the best day at work I've had in months.

At nine in the evening I lock the door. Miss Gobbler is putting the finishing touches on a plastic pot of gold and nibbling on heart-shaped Sweet Tarts she's bought herself.

"Miss Gobbler, would like to go get a smoothie with me?"

She's blushing, her face looking like it's wrapped in red cellophane.

"Well, alright," she says. "But just one." She closes up the box of Sweet Tarts. "Sugar makes me a booger."

She's yapping away as we drive, describing her favorite forms of entertainment. By the time we pass the Smoothie Shack, she's explained the entire last season of *7th Heaven*. As we cross the city limits, she's trying to remember something funny said on the KLTE Morning Zoo Show. Half an hour later she asks, "Where are we going?" I don't answer. A few minutes later she asks me again. Again, I don't answer. We're way past the city lights when she next speaks. "I'm not frightened." I look at her, but say nothing. "Good things happen to good people." I speed up into the desert. "Answer cruelty with kindness, that's what I say." I turn off the highway onto something a little less than a road. The moon is rising. "Today's sorrow is the seeds of tomorrow." Her voice cracks a little on "tomorrow." After a mile or so I stop the car, get out and open the trunk. Amongst the junk I have a shovel and a bottle of water. No flashlight, but the moon is enough.

I start digging. She watches me from the car, her breath making small fog circles on the window, which recede, refill, recede. I keep my mind on the digging.

When the hole is deep enough I collect her from the car. She doesn't run, doesn't struggle at all. She just keeps mumbling scrambled scraps from *Chicken Soup* stories.

"And that boy grew up to be Dwight D. Eisenhower..."

I lead her to the hole and have her sit down. Again, she doesn't struggle, just more gibbering. "The kind man is the wise man, love conquers all, hold on Friday's a coming." When the first shovel full of sandy dirt lands on her lap she lets out a yelp. Then she goes quiet. More quiet than I've ever known her to be. The dirt rises. At one point she tries to stand, but I shove her back down. Once the dirt is up to her chest, standing is no longer possible. She only starts screaming when the dirt reaches her neck. A harsh, cutting scream, but I keep to my work.

Pat down the dirt so that just her head is sticking out, just her head and nothing else. The ground around her slopes in, like a four-foot-wide shallow bowl. She stops screaming now. The moon is right above us. Huge, unclean, white.

I down half the bottle of water and lay back on the pile of unused dirt just to rest for a minute.

I sleep past sunrise, past the morning cool and into the heat. When I wake, Miss Gobbler is staring at me. Oversized, wet eyes.

The scene is different in the light. Grotesque. Just a head in a bowl. And I find myself asking, who did this thing?

"Thank you for staying," she whispers. I grab the shovel and throw it in the car. I'm not leaving, not yet. Sit down behind her, relax. I don't know what time it is. Morning? Maybe. Don't know. No clock. Not sure if she has a watch, but if she does it's under. It's still. It's quiet. No buzz, no hum. A little wind, nothing more.

"I'm thirsty," she says.

"That'd be the heat," I say.

I watch. She calls out every hour or so, but I don't say anything. I just watch, watch her head get kind of twitchy, watch her nod when she falls asleep. Watch the sky and the stony horizon.

"Bug!" she screams. "Big bug. Big bug!"

It is a big one. In front of her face, and her spread apart eyes are going crossed trying to watch it. I stand and squash it. She looks up at me and I've never seen a face so grateful. Real pale, but real grateful, and with those eye, she looks like a Precious Moments greeting card.

"You saved my life," she says.

"I buried you in a hole."

"I forgive you," she says.

"What?"

"I forgive you."

"No, you don't."

"I did, earlier today. I forgave you," she gives me a sickly little smile. "It's like it never happened."

"But it did happen. It's happening."

"Not in the eyes of God."

I bend down, lean in close, and flick her on the nose. "You're still in a hole."

She gazes around. This argument seems to stump her.

I sit down. More hours go by. It's a beautiful spot, really. So large and quiet. I'm just sitting watching the occasional cloud. I don't think I've ever felt so relaxed.

Sometime in the late afternoon she speaks. "I'm thirsty," she says. "I miss Yoo-hoos."

I chuckle. "Yeah. I kind of miss Slim Jims."

"Oh my, Slim Jims," she says and tries to giggle, but the thirst and weight of sand against her chest slows and grizzles the giggle into a lower laugh. It's nice.

"I miss Cheetos," she says.

"And yogurt."

"And Ding Dongs."

"We could have lived for a year with all the shit in that place."

"It was a garden."

Then she's quiet and so am I.

The sun sets. Like SunnyD and Robitussin spilling on the sky. The air changes, smells larger, as if the colors are sending their own air and there's no AC unit to protect me. This happens every day?

"Check out that sky," I say. Miss Gobbler lets out a little gasp, but nothing more.

Blue, darker than Eckerd's blue, soaks from the east.

I lay down on my back, my head beside hers and we watch each star pop into view, like Christmas lights a million miles away. More and more until the sky is nearly full. And what was quiet in the day is now a deeper, wider silence. Before there was sky, but now there's all of space.

"Do you know any of their names?" I whisper.

"No," she whispers back.

"So beautiful."

"Beautiful," she says.

"I think that red one is Mars," I say.

Her mouth opens and a high wavering voice escapes. "Mars ain't the kind of place to raise the kids. In fact, it's cold as hell."

I join in. "And there's no one there to raise them if you did."

We sing every song on that 90-minute tape, starting with "Rocket Man" and finishing off with Belinda Carlisle's "Heaven on Earth". Then we lay still, my forehead just touching her cheek. The moon rises slowly, that same dirty white.

"Thirsty," she says.

I grab the bottle of water and kneel next to her.

"Yoo-hoo?" she asks.

"Yes. Yoo-hoo." She laps it up, making little snarling noises, till the bottle is empty.

"Better?" I ask. She doesn't say anything. Just breathes.

I lay back, watch the moon. Every so often she moans a little. Once she laughs, a weird laugh, as if she just got a joke someone told her years ago. I stroke her hair and it soothes her. She's quiet. Everything is.

My mind is floating and the sky is moving. Blue clouds glowing, hiding the stars. It feels good to be alone with her, away from everything. There's no one else in the world, just her and me. It's nice. No lie. This is true. Even these raindrops feel good, water falling on my face, water wetting her hair, water trickling in the sand between us.

OF
ALL
PLACES

California

Sun, hiding behind those mountains like some shy child. Holy.
It'll make you sing. And in my rearview mirror I can see the
leftover slice of moon. Three hours since dawn. Forty hours
till Texas.

Sunlight in the morning is like liquid. It fills up the car
with that orange-yellow morning glow till you think you can
swallow it.

Yesterday I was in Santa Cruz with my brother, drinking a bot-
tomless cup of coffee and all hopped up on the songs rolling
from the speakers. My brother was telling me about a job he
had for me selling barrels.

"People need barrels," he said. "It pays well."

I roll down the car window just to get more sun in and feel the temperature change—mile by mile and minute by minute. All that change in one day.

"You can stay on the couch."

I put down my coffee, leaned back and looked up. On the ceiling of the coffee shop people had stapled dollar bills, each with a message: I LOVE MARCI, CLASS OF '03, NO WAR. And right above my head a dollar bill told me, YOU'VE GOT TO GO TO TEXAS. I looked back at my brother who was drawing a barrel on a napkin. "I've got to go to Texas, want to come?"

Maybe he's selling barrels right now. First barrel of the day. But I'm driving.

Nevada

My stereo is a soundtrack for the landscape and I'm thinking, were these girls seeing this drive when they played this song, when they put all that sad in their sound, when their voices spun around each other like lovemaking? They must have been here. Must have smelled that hot sun thawing out the pines.

Top of the ridge, twisting along. Look. You can see for years from here.

Wind drowning out my singing so I can sing all the louder, and I'm glad for the downhill, cause during the climb I was afraid the car would die out and I'd have to slide back down backward, maybe all the way back to the Pacific.

If God is cruel then he can't see me right now. I've escaped and I'm driving. If God is good then I might be the center of all things.

Utah

The car wants to stay in Utah. Ten miles from the state line, but it won't move anymore. The ground is so dry my pee disappears as soon as it hits the dirt. Thirsty earth. I wish I had something for you. All that pee, just gone. Amazing. How much pee would it take to make a puddle?

It's frightening the way the cliffs have been carved. It's like artifacts of a race of giant artists. All sculpted, a rock hard sand castle, brown-orange and lonely. The sky is high and far. The cliffs are old. In Utah everything stretches up, out, back, and I find me nowhere but now and alone. It's a good lonely, still hurts, still hollow, but being lonely in a beautiful place is finer than being lonely on my brother's couch. It's kind of a scary lonely. I'm worried it might get me. Especially when the sun goes down. If you get lonely enough God will meet you there. I'm afraid to try.

When the lonely gets this big and thick, I usually drive for a few hours, outrun the sad and find a different place, but the car wants to stay in Utah.

I wonder if any human has ever pissed on this exact spot before.

I try to sit and breathe. I love that sound. Breath. Teach me to breathe. Susan could breathe. Susan was incredible. Bleach blond dreadlocks and eyes like glacier ice. She had these tiny breasts. So tiny and round that it made me happy every time I saw them.

Close your eyes. Keep them closed, she'd say. Keep them closed for so long that the light is different when you open them again. You sit still long enough, and you listen, but you don't sleep, you listen. It's hard to do. You want to open your eyes, or you get hungry and sleepy, like your body or your brain doesn't want you to listen. So you fool your brain by making it concentrate on breathing. While your brain is busy with that the rest of you can listen.

I hear wind, a lizard, a buzz, and nothing at all. So which one is God? Listen.

Lizard, hawk, fly, pollen, and buzz. The lizard hides in the rocks as soon as I move my head, never letting me look and study and know it. The hawk is always above me, watching me, hunting me. Only its shadow touches me. The fly is in my ear, annoying me, tickling me, far too close. The pollen is silent. I only hear the wind that carries it, almost invisible, connecting everything, giving life where it lands. The buzz is in my head. No one else hears it. It might be mine and mine alone. It might drive me mad.

I don't know God's name.

Colorado

Thank you for coffee, for truck stops, for Pete who drives without speaking more than three words, for rain, for the slow climb of mountains, the new air of Colorado, pancakes, paperbacks, and coffee again.

Pete buys me a beer in a near-empty bar and tells me that if he could be anywhere in the world, he'd be young. I laugh. He buys me another beer and waves goodbye. He's heading north, not to Texas. I sit till closing, because I don't want to have to find a place to sleep. Concrete and diesel and cool wind. The beer wears off, leaves my brain sticky.

Anywhere in the world, he'd be young.

New Mexico

A car picked me up at a gas station. Woman in her thirties, plump and pretty, she kept touching her hair and trying to giggle. She lit a cigarette and cracked the window, the wind squeezing in, sucking out, like the car's a lung. She flicked the last little coal and it went a bouncing. Rolled up the window and asked me about my first time with a girl. Told me she'd never been with a man. I said that was no big deal and we were quiet for a long time. Then she stopped the car where there was no town and asked me to get out. "I want to be alone now," she said and drove off.

So now I'm walking. Long road, lights swipe by and snag the dark. Step away from the road to see more stars, to feel less steel. Walk. Catch that stride. Each step sending ripples that go on until there is no on to go on to. China hears my steps. Each step is changing the vibration, changing the world. Change the world. Walk. Like Shams walking out of the desert and finding Rumi. Like Miles walking through bee bop and finding cool. Like me getting high on coffee beans at 2 AM and walking the coast. But this is desert. Stone. Sand. All I want is this walk.

Still dark. Too late to know the time. Coming to a town, now. Homes on a golf course in the desert. Rich people sleeping with the lights on. Then, farther in, streets and a supermarket and a Baptist church with a parking garage. Buildings with no lights. Pass a man who smells like smoke and dirt. Looks like a father. Tells me I shouldn't be out so late, it might rain. It's these nights when it should be cooler because the sun went down, but it isn't, and the sky is purple and low and feels like it might rain, but it won't. I walk way too far on these nights. I think about the girl I didn't make love to, I think about being lonely, I think about losing God in god giving and god sharing and I think about the homeless guy on the yellow bike, and the poet who used to get free coffee at Cups until he died and now you can't find his books anywhere.

Across the street, a huddle of girls just getting home. Stepping inside. Giggling. Pink flesh, tight and round and curves and all flavored. Who wants to be a monk and give up all this holy lust? My want changes the weather. Humidity goes up in the whole town just because I'm hungry for her, almost any her. Maybe I should call out, ask them if they know God's name.

I used to know. Someone told me what name to call him by, how to know him. A loving God. A hunting God. ...*And we, who with unveiled faces...new creation...love that surpasses knowledge....* A serious God.

I fell in love with God and then I fell in love with a girl who taught kindergarten Sunday school at church and sometimes sang with the high school choir. One front tooth overlapped another. She split her radio listening between country and Christian stations. She collected beanie babies. She was perfect.

The girl I never made love to. And she was lying in the hallway. We had been together for over a year, touching, kissing, searching, and then praying for forgiveness. Maybe it was a game, pushing the line. But sometimes God was in the room watching, or the husband I imagined she'd someday have, watching, and we would pull away, sick, feeling a guilt as strong as pleasure. All we didn't do because we loved God. Loved God so much. And God wanted us pure.

Her grandfather died, her mom's dad. We drove five hours to the funeral. I held her hand while she cried. Huge sobs, like choking.

A good man. A Christian. Ran the good race set before him.

She was going to sing his favorite hymn, but couldn't. She was crying too much. Gulping air through the tears.

Her parents stayed with her grandmother and she and I drove the five hours back. She slept. Stretching out across the bench seat of her parents' Oldsmobile with her head on my leg. Soft hair, a little less than brown. So sad. Deep, slow breathing. I tried to match my breathing to hers.

An hour from home, she woke up. We laughed and sang along to a tape. She said she wished she could have sung the hymn, but she knew he'd understand.

It was late when we got to her neighborhood.

"You should stay," she said.

"Yeah," I said.

We were quiet for the last few miles, feeling the empty house waiting. Walking in. No one else near. Turn on a light. Have a soft drink.

She took a shower. A long one. And I waited. She came out with a towel. There was steam coming off her skin. Baby powder smell and a different smell, a spicy smell. She loosened the towel. Smiled with one tooth overlapping another, laughed, then serious. Taking the towel off, more steam from parts I'd never seen, she stood and let me watch. Lying down in the hallway between her room and the shower room. My breathing was fast. Hers was slow. Looking at me. Adult eyes. Asking eyes. Not afraid, willing.

I giggled. Turned my head. Stepped back. When I looked again I saw her eyes hurting, not understanding, me giggling in nerves. She covered herself. She didn't move at first, but her body closed. I was ashamed. Her arms folded over her chest. No more steam. She stood. Wrapping her towel around her. She went into her room. She's married now. She's in Oregon. She has babies. She's in the hallway. She's asking. I'm giggling. Jesus, that was my worst moment. My worst, Jesus. When I remember too much I want to sleep, lose it all for a while. But I'll walk instead.

Texas

Dawn. The sky is coming alive. Black to red to blue. Steps away from Texas. I can see the sign welcoming me, a picture of a flag frozen in wave. I can see the air and light is different across that line. Thanks for the air. Thanks for my legs feeling the road. Thanks that I'll step into Texas, not roll. You have led. I have followed. And all I have found is that I have followed and love you more for it. I thought I'd be leaving sad, but I just found more. Collecting sad faces and carrying them into Texas.

You are a mute trickster, you are promise, you are the hawk and lizard and fly and buzz, you are Pete and a smoking woman and pollen, you are hills and sand and a girl in a towel. You have no name and you have all names.

Today I'll call you Texas. Tonight I'll call sleep prayer. Tomorrow I'll walk some more.

LAZARUS
DYING

"Maybe he will return today," John says. He is standing by the window, trying to peek at the sky above New York's buildings. He has not put his tie on yet.

"It will not be today."

"Maybe it will be."

John starts cleaning. Shuffling around straightening cushions and the one houseplant.

"Have you seen my pamphlets?" he asks.

After John's shift at the copy shop, he hands out tracts around the city. Simple little books describing the pains of hell and the grace of the cross.

"They were on the counter this morning."

"Never saw them," I say.

They have illustrations so that even the illiterate might be saved.

"If you see them will you place them on my mat?"

"Of course."

I burn his tracts in the sink as often as I can.

I try not to watch him scurry around. I'm learning to rot.

Two thousand years ago, I was a miracle.

The first thing Jesus said to me when I stumbled from the tomb was, "I wanted to see what four days would do, Lazarus."

I nodded and brushed some flakes from my skin. He smiled and rested a hand on my back.

"I think I'll keep it to three," he said.

Pilgrims visited. They'd wait in the shade of a palm tree I planted as a young man. One by one, for a small fee, they would be led by my sisters behind a curtain to see me and ask questions. Some wanted to ask me about Jesus. Most wanted to ask me about death.

"It was nothing at the time," I told them. "In memory it is a little like biting into an under-ripened fruit, only not just your mouth, your whole body."

People didn't like this answer. They would grimace, drop a coin in Martha's hand, and head back home. Sometimes a hundred miles away. A hundred miles to find out the afterlife was not yet ready for picking. So I made up different answers.

"There is milk there. There is cheese. It is morning always." Or "Your mother is there. She complains about you constantly. Already the dead are sick of your name."

Once I told a man, "Your brother blames you for his death."

"I had nothing to do with it," he answered.

"Perhaps you wished it." I said. "So you might have his wife."

"I married her out of custom."

"He visits your room at night. Your brother watches."

I don't know why I said these things. After this man left, Martha brought me a plate of food. Olives and bread. But I could not eat it.

"The food is sick, Martha."

"The food is fine, brother. You are sick," she said. "You need to rest. To sleep."

"I cannot sleep."

"Goodnight, brother."

I could hear Mary and Martha discuss me.

"He is different. He stares," Martha said.

"He is alive. Is that not enough for you?"

"We were wrong to ask for this."

"He is a miracle."

"He frightens me."

If I was sick, when would I be healthy? The mold did not heal. And no new mold grew. Nothing changes. Until now. Now I'm rotting. I'm learning to die.

"Will you clean up a little today? he asks, tightening his tie.

"No," I say, sitting still against the wall. Our apartment is one room and one bathroom. John has purchased simple furniture. I refuse to use it, except to hide his preaching bible or holy textbooks.

John lights candles in the morning. "I prefer the soft light," he tells me. At night John pretends to sleep. He lies still with his eyes closed for hours and hours. He pretends to be hungry at meals. He reads all the scholarly books on the "historical Jesus." He claims it's devotion. In truth he wants to see how history is treating him.

"Revelations is popular again," he tells me. "Must be nigh."

"Nothing is nigh."

John is not like me. He was never dead. Never died. You can read about it in his gospel, but John swears that the story has been skewed.

"Peter and I were debating, we were always debating," John told me. "Peter said he would die for Jesus. I said the greater challenge was to live for him. Jesus heard our talk and granted us both our desires. Me, I live until he returns and Peter was crucified head down. I saw it. Saw Peter scream. But I'm still here. Jesus said we'd compare thoughts at the end of time. He said that. This won't last forever."

"Jesus was a liar."

"Never say this. Why do you say this?"

I tug at my ear. It comes off in my fingers.

"You are letting this happen," he says.

I smile. Bit by bit, I'm learning the secret. It is not trying to die, it is forgetting to live. Every day, forgetting. It is difficult. Two thousand years to learn. But look at me rot. Give me time and I'll be gone.

After my grave, the cattle feared me, wouldn't let me near. Martha did my work. I missed working. Missed coming home tired and pleased. I remember, before dying, coming home to find Jesus sitting on my floor, my sisters doting on him. Martha with her foods and annoying hospitality. Mary with her submission. If he had touched either of them, they would have filled my home with sweat, they would have disappeared through their pores. This young-eyed lust of unmarried girls.

I walked in and Martha handed me a bowl to wash my face.

"Hello, Teacher," I said.

"Hello friend," he said, "Sit. Have some wine and let's talk."

I laughed. Jesus could have the company of magicians and rich men, but he chose to sit with me. And he laughed. All his philosophy, all his teaching had laughter in it. Just below the words.

Jesus came to Bethany once more after my grave. A meal was planned at Simon the Leper's home. Martha asked me to stay away.

"There is still a smell to you brother. It will upset the Master."

I sat outside by a window, leaning on the dirt wall. I heard the laughter. I heard the eating. They could smell me through the window. I heard the complaining. It must have been strong. Mary smashed her perfume to cover the stench. She poured it out on Jesus. But Jesus was not fooled. He spoke of death.

"John, bring me back some cigarettes. I'm going to take up smoking."

"You tried that before. It didn't work."

"I'm going to try again."

Do not sleep for a year and you will remember things that never were. Do not sleep for ten years and you will mumble wisdom, cough poetry, and understand none of it. Do not sleep for a thousand years and God and Satan will dance in your throat.

I have not slept in two thousand years. My head is more blood than brains. You can hear the slush.

News came of Jesus' death. My sisters wept, tore at their breasts.

"Brother, brother. The Master is dead."

But I did not cry. And I could see they now thought of me only as a monster. Love was gone. Even pity was gone. I went back behind my curtain and stayed there.

Days later there came news of the body being gone. Of Peter seeing something.

"Peter sees what he wants to see," Martha said. "Always has."

"John saw him too," said Mary.

"John will see whatever Peter tells him to see."

"Martha, it could be true," Mary said. "Look at our brother."

"I do not want that to be true."

Curiosity grew. More pilgrims came to me every day.

But I lied about Jesus, too. I told some he was a demon. Some I told that he was a Roman spy. I told one man that Jesus gave me life so he could share my bed. This man shook his head. "I knew it," he said. "I always knew it."

Again, I don't know why I said these things. I tried to love as I loved before. My sisters, my God. But there was no love.

Soon Mary and Martha turned the pilgrims away. My sisters didn't like my answers. They didn't like the way I tried to touch the women or how I bit at the men. They told the pilgrims I was sick or asleep or visiting the Temple. I could hear them whispering, offering figs for the journey home.

Today, like most days, John will preach on the sidewalks and in the subways. Most people ignore him.

"They search for parking spaces with more urgency than they search for God," he once said.

In the poorer neighborhoods John preaches to junkies and the insane. The gangs know John. When they catch him they tie him up and urinate on him. He comes home smelling. He returns the next day with the same words, the same message. "Where you fear there is judgment, where you hope there is nothing, in that place there is actually love." They grab him again. He doesn't fight. They take his clothes and send him away naked. He believes he's doing God's work.

"You're deceived," I tell John as he gathers his scriptures and goes to the door.

"I am happy. You are not," he says while counting his keys. "Which tree drinks the true water, the strong or the withered?"

"No parables. That's the rule. None."

"It was a metaphor."

"It was very close to a parable," I say.

"You're without hope. You are rot."

"You'll be the last, you know. There'll be no believers in the world."

"You said that a thousand years ago." He closes the door behind him.

I am glad he's gone. The silence helps. I can rot away to nothing today. Perhaps today.

One evening I peeked from behind my curtain. Mary was sewing the hem of the dress she was wearing. She was smiling.

I wanted to sit with her. I would say nothing. I would touch nothing. Just sit near and watch her sew. I tried to remember being in this place, before. Could that be true again? Couldn't I sit still with my sister? I stepped through the curtain. She looked up. Her face stretched in fear.

"Mary," I said. She stood quickly, dropping the needle.

"Martha is at the market. She'll be home soon," she said. I moved forward. She stepped back into a wall. "She'll be home soon."

When I was dying Mary sat with me through the night. She dipped a cloth in water and cooled my forehead. I was sick with fever, often asleep, but each time I opened my eyes, Mary was there. "Shhh, brother. Peace," she had said. How I wish she would say this now. Cool my head now. But I was no longer her brother. I could see that in her fear. I looked down at my hands, my blue skin. I hated it. I wanted to be dead. I wanted to be mourned, not feared.

I waited without moving. She didn't move either. Then I screamed. She fell to her knees and covered her face. She didn't see me leave.

That night I tried to die. I tied a rope around my neck and hung myself from a tree. I choked and spat, but I did not die. Thieves came and stole my sandals. I kicked at them and tried to yell, but the rope only allowed me to croak. They laughed and pushed me. They left me swinging. At dawn the rope snapped and I dropped to the dust. I wept because I could not die. The dying part of me had died the first time. So I went for Jesus. I wanted him to undo what he had done. He would grant me that.

I asked wherever I went, but people were afraid. Of me and my mold. Of the Romans and the priests.

I was lonely. I bought some time in a woman's tent. The air was thick with oils. She rolled over me. I didn't move. She kissed and rubbed. She moaned like a goat but with no help from me. I asked if I could leave.

"Still the same price."

I dropped a coin and crawled over pillows to the door. But turned before I left.

"Did you see the Master when he passed through?" I asked.

"Which one?"

"Jesus of Nazareth."

"The one they killed? Yes. I saw him. His disciples kept me busy for days."

"Him as well?"

"Once. But he was like you."

I cannot remember all the things he said. Sitting on mats, talking into the dark until even Mary would yawn. Something about a kingdom and bread. Something about losing and finding, about a bad son forgiven, and a nagging widow, and buildings crumbling and stars falling and all things made new.

I came to Jerusalem, crowded and tall. I wore long robes to hide my skin. I found rumors. Jesus and Isaiah had been seen perched on the Temple's top, crying for the city. Peter had performed miracles in the name of Roman gods. The priests had stolen the Master's body and keep it in crypts under the Temple.

Many had claimed to see him.

"We saw him," one man told me. A man I knew from before. "But we didn't know it was him until he was gone."

"He has changed?"

"Yes, but...but not like you. He is *less* flesh now."

Peter could be found preaching loudly in city squares. I went to hear him and ask him to tell where Jesus was, but when I saw him I was frightened. Too bold for me to trust. He argued with everyone. His words, all his words, were flavored with argument.

I traveled for two days to Nazareth, hoping Jesus might be there with his mother. Dew forming on my beard at night. Sun in my eyes at day. I had once loved dawn, loved the gold in the palms. Nothing now.

Jesus' mother met me at the door. I knew her, but she didn't seem to know me. Too sad to know anyone. She was old. She had never been old before.

"I'm looking for your son," I said. She nodded and covered her nose. She led me to an inner room. There, scribbling by a weak candle, was John.

"Your son?" I asked her again. She nodded again and left. John looked up and let his eyes focus. He smiled. "She's my mother now, Lazarus. A gift from the Lord to her and to me."

Poor Mary. John was no Jesus. Thin, weak, and with a sad beard. Once at my home, before the deaths, Peter had slapped John's back and laughed loudly. "Looks as if an old dog has shed on your chin." All the disciples had laughed. John had smiled slightly. He was the youngest of Jesus' men. He kept close to Peter, listening as much as Peter talked. But this John was different.

"I need to find the Master," I said.

"I would have thought you'd come sooner."

"Where is he?"

"He knew you were sick. Did you know that? He waited. Said it was for God's glory. We said he should hurry."

"Please tell me how to find him." My voice was stern.

"He let you die. You have a reason." I moved close to him. "He is gone," John said.

"Where?"

"Into the sky. To Heaven to prepare a place for us. He'll return. You may wait with me, if you wish."

I turned to leave.

"I have a reason too," he said. But I didn't stay.

I was hungry for death. Life felt wrong. I needed to feast on what I had only tasted. I knew I couldn't have my own, but I could be close to others'. I returned to Jerusalem and watched the crucifixions outside the city wall. Sat near as they tied the men to the beams. Moved closer after the crowds left. Horrible. But I wanted it.

For a time I met with the church in Ephesus. Sipped wine with them. Sang hymns. Listened as they retold stories and argued about what each meant. I tried to find hope where they found hope. I could not. When Jerusalem had a famine, I volunteered to help. I wanted to see more dying. Wanted death.

I saw the city fall forty years after he called me from the cave. Everything burning and the Temple falling. I thought that this must be the end. His return. All things would be made new. But he did not return.

It's raining in New York. I stand by the window and listen, gently pulling teeth from my mouth. John will stay in the rain. He will raise his voice over thunder and speak of a love. He will return and bring me food. He eats and expects me to as well. He, like me, doesn't need food any more than he needs sleep. But John believes this is how one should live.

"John, you are so dull," I told him. "Why did Jesus put up with you?"

"He loved me."

"So you keep saying, but why?"

"Because he did."

Below the window children are playing in the puddles. My mouth does not bleed.

After Jerusalem fell, the Romans tried to burn me. I felt the pain, but my skin only bubbled. It did not burn. So they set me out on the sea with no sail and no supplies. The sea didn't kill me either. For days and months I floated, watching the blue above and the blue below until my eyes changed hue. Eventually my boat fell to planks and I floated free, on my back, up and down on waves like small mountains. Staring at the sun, which crossed the sky as if blown by the wind. Fish kissed my palms and jumped over my face. Always waves in my ears and salt in my skin.

Sometimes I was afraid. The sky seemed to be moving farther and father away. At night I would hear howling and see shadows rise up larger than the Temple. I believed all the world was again flooded. No one but me remained.

Other times my fear was like awe. Sky, sea, and stars. I sang Psalms and worshipped. The stars were like souls. The children of Abraham. The salt in my eyes and the spray in the air would catch moonlight and make it seem as if perhaps the stars were finally falling. I had been promised they would fall and all things would be made new.

The stars did not fall. They don't fall. They fade. Every

morning, they fade. For two thousand years, they do nothing but fade.

After a year I floated on to a green coast. Light skinned people found me, carried me to a bed with wool blankets. Dried my skin and poured oil over my scalp. They spoke, but I didn't understand. One woman, wearing fur, took warm water and washed my face. She hummed and I knew the melody. A Psalm. And behind her stood John.

"John?" I asked.

"God is good. He has brought us here."

"God is God. And I am no man to judge if he is good."

"Your eyes have changed, Lazarus."

"It was the sea."

"Nothing has changed with me."

I stayed with him in Gaul. He the vocal, the minister; I the quiet, the monk. Both serving. It was good. But after many years we both felt driven to move on. For John it was too much to stay a generation and watch each baby born grow old and die. For me, it was the old hunger. John went looking for life. I sought death.

"There is a reason you and I do not die," he told me as we said goodbye. "We are chosen to witness. 'He will not let his servant know the corruption of the grave.'"

"My heart is not like your heart, John."

"We will find each other again. We always will. Like brothers. You and I are children of the same miracle."

By the wall where I sit, John has a box of tiny green bibles that he hands out to neighbors and schoolchildren. He gave me a bible once. A large one with a leather binding. John said that the engraving on the front was my name. I can't read.

"Tell me again how he died," I asked, rubbing the leather along the spine with my thumbs.

"Confusion, people screaming at him. He spoke kindness even then."

"Was there much blood?"

"Yes," he said and cringed. "He asked God to forgive them."

"Could you see his pain? Tell me about that."

"Why do you ask these things? And be careful with your bible. You're twisting it," he said.

"Did you see him after?" I asked. "When the tomb was empty?"

"Once. From a distance. He was on shore. I was in Peter's boat."

"That's it?" I felt the spine of that bible thin in my hands. It would snap easily.

"Others saw him."

"Oh, John."

The children are still playing below the window. I would throw bibles at them until they run away. They'd return with eggs. This happens nearly every day. But today I am letting go of each speck of skin, each mote of dust. I let go. It is slow. Life holds on and I am still here. I would like John to come home and find only a puddle. What have I not let go? What am I holding?

After Gaul, John went to the living. Spoke of Christ to crowds. Sowed mercy. Built churches in each town that would let him. People marveled at his patience, his long suffering.

I went to the dying. Leper colonies, battlefields, hospices. People believed me merciful.

"He stays with them to the end," they said of me. "Holds their hands, strokes their hair. A saint."

I once helped a child die. I was tending the sick and dying in a plague clinic. Hungry to be close to their death since I was so far from my own. This child, a boy, had a growth in his neck that was closing his throat. A slow strangle. Pain with every moment. Killing him seemed like it would be such a tiny act. I would steal some days, maybe hours, from him, that's all. I tried believing it was mercy. I put my hand over his nose and mouth. He kicked and watched me. Then he closed his eyes tight and I flicked his forehead with my finger saying, "Open them, open them," until he did.

God did not stop me. I had expected he would still my hand. But God stayed away. He would not let me die, but he allowed me to kill. Worse. In the sickness of the act, God had hidden pleasure. It brought me no closer to death. It was more like life.

I cursed God that day. I went to cities so that He would not find me.

I saw the Church grow. Heard John's name, Peter's name, even my own. Wood churches became stone. Stone churches became cathedrals. I visited these to see images of my sisters in clothes and landscapes they had never seen. There, too, was Jesus. Beaten, bloody, and royal. But I saw no sign of his kingdom. I saw Jews murdered in Prague. Blacks sold in London. Women raped in Istanbul. Rome was called holy. Rome was never holy.

In Paris a thief with one eye beat me, wanting me dead. He stabbed me and cried when I didn't bleed. I told him I was sorry. In other cities, at other times, I had whips against my back. Stones tied to my legs. My survival meant nothing.

I watched cities fill the air with smoke. Buildings stab clouds.

I made my way to New York and was living under a bridge watching old drunks die of cold. I sat by them, counted their last breaths, watched the mist above their lips. Some reached for my hand. Some pretended I was their father. I was known. They came from all over the city, like the pilgrims had come before. But they had no questions. Just wanted someone near to help with the dying. You see, I believed I desired dying. But dying is an act for the living. I desire death.

"Like falling asleep," I told them. "As easy as that."

I kept the bodies in a hole cut into the banks of the river. When the hole was nearly full I crawled in among them and imagined I had found Sheol. I lay flat. In the day there was light enough to see the faces. Drawn, rotting, bearded. I spoke to them as if these were my ancestors. *Here we are. Here we are.* But I did not die. I did not change. At night I laid still and made no noise. When it rained, muddy water dripped from the soil above and the wind groaned.

John found me there, playing dead. Pulled me by my feet into the air. I tried to crawl back in. But John held my legs. I refused to use my muscles, so he lifted me like a child. Strong arms for a man so thin. He carried me onto a bus. I kept my eyes closed, but could hear the doors open, the engine rumble below us. He hummed a little. Said my name into my ear. The heat of his breath, the heat of others on the bus burned more than the Roman flames.

The bus stopped and he carried me again. John carrying a corpse through the streets, but no one asked. He carried me like the sea had carried me. I floated. He carried me up the stairs, stumbling only once. Inside he laid me on his mat and drew a bath. There was steam and more heat. He made a tea that smelled of spices and put it to my lips. I didn't drink. Tea dribbled down my chin.

Through all of this I did not think. I was doing my best to be dead.

He dried me with a towel and dressed me in a robe.

I still did not open my eyes or speak a word. John read to me. *Charlotte's Web, The Little Prince, Mother Goose.* He used different voices for each character. His women sounded shrill. His villains sounded Roman. He hummed and sang. He combed a century's worth of knots from my hair.

His actions were a comfort and a chastising. Without words he was saying, "You cannot pretend to be dead. That is not your lot."

One day he filled a bowl with warm water and washed my feet. I could hear him sing.

"God, you are good. Sweet Lord, you are good."

"God is God," I said. My first words in months. "Who can say if He's good?"

"You and I are here," he said, pausing his washing. "That is evidence."

"Survival isn't evidence." I looked down at him.

"That is not what I meant," he said and returned to my feet.

John comes home in the half-light of evening. His eyes are tired. Red snakes in the white. He moves slowly, loosens his tie and stretches his neck. I am sitting against the wall, just as he left me. My legs no longer move. He cannot see how little of me is left. He sits on a stool near me.

"They do not listen, Lazarus," he says. "Starving children laughing at the food I offer." His voice has tears in it. "It is not enough to live for them. It is not enough that he died for them. Nothing will open their eyes."

"John," my mouth is toothless. "Where are my cigarettes?"

"I smoked them."

"Where is my food?" I ask.

"No more food for those who won't eat. No more."

He lies down on his mat. Still determined to pretend he can sleep. He will rise early and pray. He will go back to those who can hurt a man who cannot die. He is tired. Young John. Troubled John. You're going to lose him, Jesus. What will you do if even he leaves you?

"John," I say, my words sound like mush.

He breathes deeply. He pretends so well sometimes I believe he is asleep. He believes he is asleep. Perhaps he is.

"John?" I say.

He breathes and says nothing.

I lay down against the wall. From here I can see the sky, darker every moment. My eyes are going. Dripping from my head. I cannot see the stars. They could be falling and I'd never know.

"John," I say. "Perhaps tomorrow he will return."

He only breathes.

Come, Lord Jesus. For his sake, come soon.

GOODNIGHT

At night, when the wife is asleep, I sneak across the street to the funeral home and whisper through the air conditioning vents. "Hello, dead people," I say. "They solved all the problems today," I say. "God gave up the job and we voted Ms. Mayfield, the kindergarten teacher, as the new God. Remember her? Smiled at every drawing you gave her. Read books aloud, holding up each page for everyone to see. She never told when you soiled your pants, just helped you clean up. She said special things happen. She blinked those big brown eyes and promised she loved each of us. She made sure that every kid in class won Show and Tell at least once—even the boy who didn't speak English and kept bringing the same glass paperweight every week. She's God now, and everything is sweet and we have naptime and cookies and cubbies and learn new things and when we're good we get stars by our name—but real stars now, because she's God. And when we mess up, she takes us aside and talks to us, puts us in Time Out for a few minutes, and we learn our lesson. And remember how she smelled like cotton sheets right out of the dryer? Now the whole world smells like that. And Ms. Mayfield smiles at us as she floats in all places at once. Life is so very good. But you're dead. Ha. Bad timing. HA!"

Then I sneak home, before the sprinklers come on, crawl into bed and bite my mattress till my gums bleed.

LISH

Lish was going to die. She was only twenty-two and beautiful. She smelled of sandalwood and tea. She couldn't sit through a full movie unless it was a musical or science fiction. She wasn't convinced time existed. She believed bubbles, stars, and poems were all the same thing. Trees said her name, *Lish*. So did sidewalk puddles and passing busses, *Lish*. She had broken her nose in a swimming hole at the age of sixteen and loved the crooked arc that remained. Lish believed that if she wanted to have a baby she need only nod. Lish's body hummed. It was happy to belong to her and she was happy to have it. But that wouldn't last for long, because Lish was going to die.

> *~Excuse me*
>
> *~Yes, Lish.*
>
> *~Nothing dies. Energy is never destroyed, just changed.*
>
> *~Then you won't mind when a painting of the British Fleet defeating the Spanish Armada falls on your head.*

Lish was walking through the park, watching squirrels chase each other around an oak tree with thick, drooping branches. She liked the picture, these grandparents of nature shrugging as the younger members of the world scurried through their limbs.

The way the squirrels hopped and scrambled had Lish thinking about the sperm swimming around her plump eggs. She thought of her high school love, Brinkley. It had been five years since she had seen him, but Brinkley's sperm would still be waiting. Brinkley had been stout and strong, a wrestler. She pictured his sperm having a similar build, shoving their way past Professor Hoggles' snobby, middle-aged sperm (two years ago), or Pev's sperm (last spring) that were so stoned they were probably just finding her fallopian tubes. Of course, Belinda didn't leave any sperm (Halloween night), just pleasant memories and lipstick stains.

Sometimes Lish felt sorry for the sperm, waiting and wanting. She was tempted to just nod her head and let them go for the egg. But Lish wanted just one more competitor. His name was Rex H.

She had never met Rex H, never seen his face except for the faded image on a flyer that had wrapped itself around Lish's shin a week before:

REX H, THE FAMED ASIAN HIP-HOP SLAM-POET HAS RHYMED FROM COAST TO COAST, SEA TO SEA, TO NYC TO NC TO MC TO SEE THE YOU IN YOU AND THE ME IN ME. SKIN LIKE HONEY, TONGUE LIKE A HAWK, WHITTLING THE WORLD WHENEVER HE TALK.

Below the words was a picture of a lanky Asian man with dreadlocks and eyes that reminded Lish of wet Tootsie Rolls.

Lish thought he looked silly, too serious, and beautiful. He was performing that night at Groundmeet. Lish stepped out of the park and headed in that direction.

> ~*Is that where I die?*
> ~*Yes.*
> ~*What if I don't go?*
> ~*You have to go as much as I have to write you going. If the story says you die and I let you live than I kill the story and you never get to live.*
> ~*That sounds silly.*

Thanks to intrusive roots, the sidewalk was bumpy and broken. It reminded Lish of her nose. She thought back to her swimming hole incident, back to the moment after the dive and before the pain. The moment in the water. The wet. The blurry green. The bubbles that petered from the corners of her mouth.

She often thought of bubbles. Air in a moving sojourn, traveling through the water, but always separate. Jiggling to the surface, popping out into the air-world and living as words. As poems. Then floating to the sky to become stars. All stars were once poems. All poems were once bubbles. When Lish spoke a poem she believed she was voicing bubbles and whispering stars.

"I saw stars," she told her mother after her swimming hole accident.

"Yes, oh, yes," her mother laughed. "With a smack like that, I imagine you did."

"No, I saw *the* stars."

From that day on there was seldom a time that Lish did not have a book of astronomy or physics within her reach. She read science textbooks like poetry and grew to believe that Stephen Hawking and William Blake were actually the same person. The facts she read were as full of mystery and beauty as the myths she whispered when she couldn't fall asleep. She understood the life cycle of a sun, the composition of a comet, the categories of galaxies, and she could still wish on a shooting star.

She took to lying awake most nights, watching the sky and waiting for a star to die. Would it pop and pow like the fireworks her brother used to set off in rich people's lawns? Or would it just blink away? Would she feel it go? Feel the universe a light less, even if it happened a million years before she saw it?

She was still a mile from Groundmeet, when who should step out from a Styln' Cuts? None other than Rex H.

"Hi, Rex H," she said. "I'm walking to watch you."

He turned and raised a hand to his new cut. In person he was even more beautiful than his photocopied image. He was clean, sculpted, and somehow childish.

"Who be you?" he asked, doing sign language for a "B" and a "U" correspondingly.

"Lish."

"Nice." He smiled, a pristine, white, nearly perfect smile. "And you're heading to Groundmeet? Well, I do hope to impress as I digress through all I confess. Yes, yes, and yes." As he spoke, his head swiveled like a slow-motion bobble-head doll.

Lish bit her lip.

Rex H cocked his head to one side, a dimple on his left cheek appearing. "Wants ride con me?" He motioned to a black and silver, souped-up, state-of-the-art moped.

Lish very much wanted to ride con him. She straddled the bike. The leather seat felt smooth and cool against her unveiled kwaggle. Lish owned just one pair of panties, which she wore only on Christmas and the Fourth of July.

"So sweet. You a poet? You look like a poet."

"Yes," Lish said. "I'm an astronomer."

"Nice." He revved up the cycle. Lish wrapped her arms around Rex H's waist.

The journey was delicious—the wind, the noise, the smell of Rex H's shampooed hair, the bouncing of the seat between her legs. She loved how the cycle cut ahead into time, accelerated a little faster than humans were meant to. She was an outlaw of physics.

As they rode Rex H explained his poetry. "My rhymes are sublime, amazing the mind. Ideas weave through words like wind through birds, like whey through curds, like corn through turds. Yes, indeed."

When they arrived, Rex H asked her if she'd share one of her poems. She smiled, but didn't answer. He put his hand against the small of her back and they walked in together.

Quiet boys, she said to the sperm, who were doing agitated summersaults deep within her loins.

"Butterflies?" Rex H asked.

"Not really," she answered.

Groundmeet was a punk alternative coffee shop with an all vegan menu. No light brighter than a few candles or a dim lamp touched the blood red walls. There were two windows, but both were painted over in black with the words LOOK WITHIN spray-painted on.

Lish loved the place. She loved the sawdust smell, the red velvet cushions, the ornately framed oil painting of the British Fleet defeating the Spanish Armada that hung from the high ceiling, tethered to the floor by a rope.

~Is that it?

~Yes, Lish.

~I'm not frightened.

~No?

~Write an O.

~O

~See the center.

~Yes.

~That's eternity.

~What about the outside?

~That, too.

~What about the O itself?

~It's nothing. You just made it. Like a frame floating on the ocean.

~You're still going to die.

~Now write an O and then delete it.

~Did it.

~Is the white still there?

~Yes, Lish.

~See?

~I could burn the page.

~You'd make smoke.

~I could open all the windows.

~Wind.

~I could reverse all time until things fell back into the one wrinkle before the beginning and leave everything there.

~I wish you would.

Rex H ordered two soy kolaches, and he and Lish took a seat next to the Noam Chomsky wish fountain. Lish was glad to be sitting by the bust of Noam Chomsky. Whenever she re-wrote her childhood, Noam was her father, Frida Kahlo was her mother, and they home schooled her. Stephen Hawking, who was also William Blake, was her frequently visiting uncle.

Rex H held out a nickel. "Wish?" he said and handed her the coin. She flung the coin, it bounced off of Noam's forehead and into the water.

"What, my Lish, was your sweet wish?"

Lish smiled and bit into her kolache.

Rex H leaned in close. "Tell me a poem."

She yearned for poetry, hurt for poetry. Bubbles to words to stars. But she had never shared her writings with anyone.

> ~*You've never asked to hear my poems.*
> ~*I don't need to. I'm the one who writes them.*
> ~*You really believe that?*
> ~*Yes, I do.*
> ~*Then you're a pretty shitty writer.*

"You got to partake to taste what's at stake," Rex H told her. Lish did sometimes perform her poems at home for an audience of a saltshaker and a ceramic paperweight. Lish would step onto a milk crate stage. She was always nervous while doing this, which is one of the main reasons she did it. Nothing else made her nervous, not the spelling bees she was compelled to compete in, not cheating on Professor Hoggles' philosophy tests during her one semester of college, not any dance from her two years as "Lemon" at The Red Rose Entertainment Bar and Bistro. The nervous thrill of poetry was its own distinct feeling.

She would pause, glance at the saltshaker and paperweight, and lick her lips. Then Lish would begin.

"Polly Flip." She would give the smallest curtsy and leave the stage.

Another night her poem was: "Pitten Sour."

"Come on, sweetness, let me hear one." Rex H smiled and his dimple came to life again.

"Aroma Pension," she whispered and did the best curtsy she could while sitting.

"Nice," said Rex H, leaning back. "But why so small? I mean a poem is a stack of words, a tower of words, that you can climb up on and touch the sky."

"Small flies."

Once she had tried to write a three worded poem. She got as far as "Loosely Gargle" and hit a block. For days she prayed that the third word would fall from heaven, float down like a piece of cloud and land in her pink and purple notebook. "Come on, God," she whispered. "Lend a hand." But God gave no word. Eventually she stopped waiting and considered the poem complete. When she read it, she always paused for an extra beat after "Gargle" and before her curtsy. That extra space is what made the poem special. It quickly became her favorite poem because it had been coauthored by God. She had written the words and He had written the silence.

"Hey, I got to do this performing thing." Rex H touched Lish's hand. "Can we talk more afterward?"

Lish nodded.

The crowd, thirty maybe forty, packed the place. All here to see Rex H's rising star. He had appeared on VH1, ABC's *Hot-Spot Poets,* and had even made a guest appearance on the short-lived *American Poet Idol.* And though Lish had just met him, she felt proud.

"Tell some truth now," someone said from the middle of the room. Someone else whistled.

Rex H swaggered onto the stage. His shoulders moved forward first, making big circles, and as if their momentum was enough, the rest of his body rose up the steps. The crowd went still and Rex H began.

"Hot mother fucking trivial pursuit," he slid across the stage, holding out his palms. "They have yet to film the yellow man's *Roots.*" The crowded hooted. He closed his palms. "No *Uncle Tom's Cabin.* No *Schindler's List.* Not even our own *Gorillas in the Mist.* No story about the Yellow Man, no story about me. Unless you count Jackie Chan or old dead Bruce Lee."

> ~*He's good.*
> ~*He's not that good, Lish.*
> ~*It's the energy. The emotion. It's sweet.*
> ~*It's trite.*
> ~*I think you're jealous.*

"A white satellite can see the Great Wall from space, but no white sees past my yellow face." Rex H paused, drawing the audience in with his Tootsie Roll eyes. "The reason I'm pleasin' until you people be weezin' and thinking of treason is—"

"You suck," someone yelled from the back of the room and then a few laughs.

"As I was saying…the reason I'm pleasing—"

"Boo! You're the worst stand-up ever." The voice was French, each syllable surrounded by a buttery crust.

"The reason I'm pleasing—"

"Here's a poem," the French voice said. "Go fuck a duck." More laughter and what sounded like high-fives.

Lish knew who it was. For the past several weeks the local art scene had been plagued by a cruel collection of beefed-up Dadaists.

~Beefed-up Dadaists?
~Quiet, you. I'm writing.

The gang wandered about town in pinstriped suits tight against their bulging physiques and intruded upon any expression of art. Recently they had disrupted a downtown art exhibit, two high school plays, and a midnight showing of David Lynch's *Eraserhead*.

Rex H stood perfectly still and stared into the murk in the back of the room. The crowd stiffened. The air felt cold, dangerous. Rex H stepped from the stage onto a front row table.

"Yo so French, yo snail-smacker," he said, stepping from table to table until he was in the middle of the room, eyes fixed on the thick shadows. "No soap, no hope, just wine and crackers."

One of the Dadaists stood. He was over six feet tall and built like a linebacker. His shirt had been removed and painted on his chest was the word "excrement."

"Your poems," he said, sucking on a long cigarette. "They tickle my scrotum like a well-placed piece of broccoli."

"I'll show you broccoli," Rex H said, stepping closer. The crowd cheered.

The Dadaist causally grabbed Rex H's leg. Umph—Rex H fell.

Lish watched as the Dadaist kneaded his fist into Rex H's face. She watched as a small woman flung her body onto the Dadaist's bare back. She watched as the other Dadaists and poets rose for battle. She thought about the silence God had written. "And this," she whispered.

A coffee cup smashed against Noam Chomksy's head. *And this*, she thought.

Rex H, still in a headlock, bit the Dadaist's bare belly. *And this*.

Lish noticed that Rex H and the Dadaist were glowing. *And this*.

The chairs, the tables, the small woman, the crowd, the floor, Noam's broken face, the blood red walls, the kolaches were all glowing. *And this*.

A toddler knocked over a votive candle and cried. *And this*.

A woman scooped up the child in her arms. *And this*.

The flame from the candle ate at a rope tied to bolt on the floor. *And this*.

The burning rope said, *Lish. And this*.

Someone slipped on the water from the Noam Chomsky fountain and pushed Lish against the wall. *And this*.

The rope snapped and the oil painting of the British fleet defeating the Spanish Armada plummeted toward the back half of Lish's skull. *And this*.

Lish looked up to see that the approaching frame and the rope above it were also glowing. So were her eyelashes.

And this.

Lish stepped out of the way and the frame smashed to the floor.

> ~*That was the painting. Why'd you let me live?*
> ~*I don't have to answer that.*
> ~*But you let me live.*
> ~*The story isn't over yet.*

Lish climbed up on a stool and looked out over the crowd, out over the conflict. And Lish saw her stool was a tiny stage. She was not nervous, she was not even aware of herself.

"A Poem for Peace in One Word," she said. But no one heard. The fighting raged on, more fierce, more powerful than any word. Then she spoke her poem. Her poem was a sigh, a bubble that burst. The sigh filled the room. It wet Dadaists' eyes and poets' bones. It ruffled Rex H's hair. Rex H, still in a headlock, saw her. He released the Dadaist's stomach from his mouth and smiled. And if Lish had learned to hold a moment forever, this would be the moment. She curtseyed. Rex H nodded. She looked down at the painting lying on the floor, a square of ocean, sky, and ships.

And Lish dove right into the painting…

> ~*Wait, Lish. I didn't say you could do that.*
> She jumped in headfirst. She half-expected another smack-crack but instead Lish found sky and an ocean below. As she dropped she yelled to the Spanish to turn

back before it was too late. Floating on the ocean, between two burning ships, was another frame. Lish splashed through the frame, through water for just a moment, bubbles petering from the corners of her mouth, and then she fell into another sky above another ocean. Here the air was free of cannons and gunpowder. Below her on the waves, another frame. Splash! Into a sky filled with clouds and down into another frame floating on a blue-green ocean. Splash! The water was filled with the songs of whales. Lish sang along. Then another sky. Another floating frame. Splash! Sky. Floating frame. Splash! Dinosaurs waddling and watching from the shore. Lish waved. Splash! Sky. Sickly trilobites peeking from the surf. Floating frame. Splash! Sky. Below her boiling seas…

~Lish, that's going to hurt.
~Quiet, you. I'm writing.

Splash! Underwater volcanoes with lava like fudge. Sky and another frame and the seas were black. Splash! Cold. Another frame and there were no seas at all. And Lish fell even faster, an outlaw of physics. Another frame and she fell into stars, an ocean of stars, on which floated another frame and through that an ocean of younger, bluer stars, then glowing dust like speeding lightning bugs, one light, no light, one atom, no atom, one wrinkle, one nothing that gave birth to all something and the nothing is the shape of a frame.

~*What's there, Lish?*

~*I don't know.*

~*Neither do I, so you can't go. You can't go where the writer can't describe.*

~*You really are a shitty writer.*

~*I can't follow, Lish.*

~*No need.*

~*Think of the sperm.*

~*I'm just doing what they would do. This is the kwaggle of all things.*

~*Think of Rex H.*

~*Floating frame. Nothing more.*

~*Think of me.*

~*I will.*

~

~

~

~*Goodbye.*

Goodbye.

and *this*

ACKNOWLEDGMENTS

Thanks to the excellent journals and insightful editors who helped craft and publish many of these stories: "Pierced" and "Heart Thongs for Jesus," *So It Goes: The Literary Journal of the Kurt Vonnegut Memorial Library*; "The Martyrs of Mountain Peak," *Puerto del Sol*; "Lord Baxtor Ballsington," *Word Riot*; "Christmas," *Fish Anthology 2006*; "The Beginning of All Things," "Four Tiny Tales Concerning Transformation," and "The Adventures of Stimp," *The Austin Daze*; "Of All Places," and "Lazarus Dying," *Tiferet: A Journal of Spiritual Literature*; "The Fecalist," *Blow*; "St. Gobbler's Day," *Blow* and in a slightly alerted form in *Two Note Solo*; "Lish," *Absinthe: New European Writing*.

Special thanks to my wonderful editor and wise counsel Liz Parker. And thanks to Megan Fishmann, Kelly Winton and the entire Counterpoint/Soft Skull Press family.

Much thanks goes to Matthew Bialer and Lindsay Ribar at Greenburger Associates for excellent guidance and representation.

And thanks to all those who read and commented on these stories including Ric Williams, Matt & Melissa Stuart,

Stacey Swann, Manuel Gonzales, Mike Yang, and Michael & Stephanie Noll. And much thanks to Deltina Hay for originally putting this collection in print. And thanks to the MFA Program at Texas State University and all the fine writers and teachers I had the honor of learning from while there. Thanks to Paul Cohen and his wonderful family for continued support even after seeing me naked.

Thanks, too, to my comedy colleagues—Les McGehee, John Erler, Jerm Pollet, and so many others. And to Tim and Karrie League and the Alamo Drafthouse. And thanks to Russell Sharman and Chris Mass for laughter and wisdom.

I wrote most of these stories in the cozy corners and breezy courtyards of Austin's holy coffeehouses. Thank you especially to Leslie and the crew at Bouldin Creek Cafe and Rob & Jenée and the gang at Once Over Coffee Bar.

And finally, thank you with all my heart and all my smiles to Jodi, Arden, and Oscar. I love you more than Nutella and hot tea.

ABOUT THE AUTHOR

Owen Egerton is one of the talents behind the award-winning The Sinus Show and Master Pancake Theater at the Alamo Drafthouse Cinema, and for several years was the artistic director of Austin's National Comedy Theatre. He's written screenplays for Fox, Warner Brothers, and Disney studios. He is also the author of the one-man play *The Other Side of Sleep* and the novel *The Book of Harold*, which is currently in development as a television series with Warner Bros. Television. He lives in Austin.